White Meteors and the Ghost of Sue Ann McGee is Wayne Frye's third book in the Legends Series. His first two books in the series, *How Hockey Saved a Jew from the Holocaust: The Rudi Ball Story*, and *Hockey Mania and the Mystery of Nancy Running Elk* were best sellers on Amazon. Like his Canadian mystery series featuring private-eye Aaron Adams, *White Meteors and the Ghost of Sue Ann McGee* is filled with nuanced references to the ills of society and offers a mosaic of the possibilities for a world where justice reigns supreme. It takes place in 1963 in the small town of Asheboro, North Carolina, where Frye's famous detective, Aaron Adams, is just beginning to develop his detecting skills by investigating a death that has perplexed the community for years. While doing so, this budding detective struggles with all the various elements that plague adolescents who are on the cusp of adulthood. Yet, just like the adult Aaron Adams who winds up in New York City many years later, the young Aaron trembles with indignation at any injustice and takes a bold stand against tyranny.   *Helium Review*

Although this story takes place in Asheboro, North Carolina in 1963, Wayne Frye teaches lessons that are universal, no matter what year it might be or where the story might occur. What was happening in 1963 is certainly germane to the world of today. There was war, religious intolerance, poverty, persecution of minorities and economic injustice. The wealthy and powerful still ruled with absolute impunity as they do today, but there seemed to be hope for a better tomorrow.   *Library Review*

In one of the town's cemeteries is a grave with a tombstone that reads *Sue Ann McGee, RIP*. However, the grave cannot imprison that which refuses to rest in peace. This restless spirit is about to wreck havoc on not only those who murdered her, but on others who commit mayhem in the tiny corridor where her spirit roams the local high school.   *Courier-Times*

J. Wayne Frye

TO: The Asheboro High School Class of 1963
Yes, 1963, When a Perplexing Mystery was Solved
These were the people who shared an incredible journey of discovery in a world that was changing so rapidly that they had trouble fathoming what lay ahead for them. Although some of them have passed away, the memories of those no longer here still burn brightly in aging minds. Through the years, they have all persevered, and although many of them have wandered far from home as they followed divergent paths of growth and rarely or never see each other, there shall always be an indelible, harmonious bond between them, because they shared that most precious gift, youth.

And To Ann Powell
My 12th grade English teacher. I knew her for only one year, but she showed me the power of words and how to make them a beacon of light in the darkness that engulfs a world where the many are expected to bow in supplication to the privileged few who rule with the iron fist of repression. She is truly a teacher who made a difference in my life, and the lives of all her students. I only wish I knew where she was, so I could say the most powerful word in the English language – thanks.

Catalogue Number: 20126196111

ISBN: 978-0-9879728-6-6

Distributed by
Fireside Books – Port Angeles, Washington

White Meteors
And
The Ghost
Of
Sue Ann McGee

By
J. Wayne Frye

FOR READERS OUTSIDE CANADA
Please note that all words are spelled according to the **Canadian Merriam-Webster Dictionary**; consequently, USA, UK, Australian and European teachers should explain the different spellings to their students.

The Author

Wayne Frye's Aaron Adams series has been popular among Canadian mystery lovers since first appearing in 2005. He provides satirical political commentary to many Canadian newspapers, and his books on politics have created a great deal of controversy. He has written marketing/advertising textbooks, been a successful U.S. university hockey coach, professor, university president and served as a marketing consultant to hockey teams and motion picture companies. He has been cited for his work with inner-city gang children in the Los Angeles area and been active in the anti-globalization movement. He became a Canadian citizen in 2003 and lives with his wife, Jasmine, also an author, in Ladysmith, British Columbia.

Other Fireside Books by J. Wayne Frye
Adolescent -Legends Series
Hockey Mania and the Mystery of Nancy Running Elk
How Hockey Saved a Jew From the Holocaust:
The Rudi Ball Story
Aaron Adams Series
Fall From Apocalypse
Armageddon Now
Something Evil in the Darkness at Hopkins House
When Jesus Came to Jersey as the Son of Thunder
The Girl Who Stirred Up the Whirlwind
When Jesus Came to Canada to Lead an Indigenous Rebellion
The Girl Who Danced with the Demons of Darkness (Coming Soon)
Social Awareness
The Catastrophic Calamities of a Village Idiot
Fighting for Justice in the Land of Hypocrisy
Cataclysmic Dreams in Black and White
(With Harriet Running Elk)
Reference
Guide to Alternative Education (13 Editions) ERA BOOKS
Biography
Worth
Books by J. Wayne Frye with Jasmine Falling Rain Frye
Canadian Angels of Mercy – Nurses in Times of Peril
Points of Rebellion: North American Aboriginals
Who Fought for Justice

TABLE OF CONTENTS

Downtown Asheboro, North Carolina (Circa, 1963)

**Hop's Bar-B-Q, where Aaron Adams took
Casey Felton on their first date.**

NOTE ON VOCABULARY

In order for students to obtain maximum benefit from the vocabulary in the book, it is recommended that before reading each chapter, teachers should encourage or require students to review the vocabulary words starting on page 242 that are categorized by chapter. A teacher's guide that includes questions for discussion by chapters and specific projects is available from the publisher.

DISCLAIMER

This is a work of fiction, and any similarity to persons living or dead is purely coincidental. The town of Asheboro does exist. It is located in the centre of the state of North Carolina in the USA. Its current population is approximately 25,000. At the time this story takes place, the population was probably between 7,000 (1954) and 9,000 (1963). The author of this book lived the first 18 years of his life there. In fact, it was there that Ms. Ann Powell, 12th grade English teacher at Asheboro High School, encouraged him to pursue writing as a career. She was a beacon of light that forever shines through the young people she mentored.

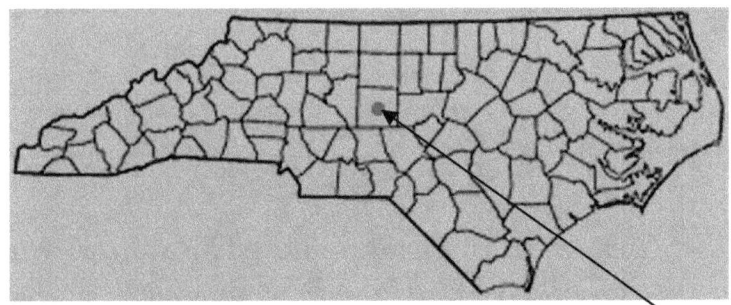

**State of North Carolina and Location of Asheboro,
Where Sue Ann McGee Met Her Death
And Refused to Rest Quietly in Her Grave**

PROLOGUE
I SHALL NOT REST QUIETLY

She floats about almost politely.
From the cold grave she creeps.
There is a chill of mischief about.
Though the earth covers her body,
She refuses to rest quietly.

Sue Ann McGee was born in 1936 to parents who were so poor they lived in a converted barn. She met her demise in 1953 while in gym class at a high school in Asheboro, North Carolina. The death was ruled accidental. It appeared that while she was climbing the grappling rope hanging from the gym ceiling, the rope, which apparently had not been checked in years, snapped in two and she plunged 30 feet to the floor, landing on her head, breaking her neck and dying instantly.

Willie Martin, the rotund, relatively incompetent chief-of-police, was not a skilled investigator, and when physical education teacher, Alene Fields, described what occurred, he pursued the investigation no further, simply stating that it was an unfortunate accident. An autopsy was performed, and it was discovered that Sue was three months pregnant. Many in the community, which was very religious and bound to tradition, looked disdainfully on what was considered, at the time, a heinous act of indiscretion on the part of a young person. Her funeral was attended by few people from the school or the community, as she was from what was euphemistically referred to as "the other side of the tracks." Of course, like so many poor people, Sue Ann's parents decided to spend excessively on their daughter's funeral, despite their meagre means.

The school's insurance company eventually gave the parents $15,000, which was considered, by many, excessive for someone like Sue, who had no potential in life anyway, as she came from poverty, and would, no doubt, according to many of the more upstanding citizens, have ended up living on the margins of society like her parents. Ironically, $12,000 of the $15,000 went to the funeral parlour, as Sue's casket was solid bronze with gold trim around the lid. As funeral parlour owner, Derrick Bodine said to Mary and Frank McGee, "in her fine dress and magnificent coffin, she will rest in luxury until the day Jesus comes back to raise all the dead and take them to glory." The distraught parents, overwhelmed with grief, mournfully agreed to make monthly payments to assure that their beloved daughter was given in death that which she had been denied in life. The $200 dress cost at least $190 more than any dress the young girl had ever worn while she was alive, but she would be going to heaven in a fine garment. Of course, little did the parents know that there was no back to the garment in order to save the dressmaker money. Even in the USA of 1953, the culture of greed was alive, well and rampant among those who ascribed to the idea customers were meant to be fleeced. Grief could be used to make money, and, after all, wasn't that what America was all about?

On the day of the funeral, as the coffin was lowered into the ground, while the minister dutifully performed the usual ceremonial incantations, a sobbing Mary McGee looked into the distance and saw a cloaked figure with the face completely covered, standing by an oak tree about 100 metres away. Whoever it was had their head bowed and seemed to be in deep sorrow. Why did he or she not come up and join the others by the graveside, thought Mary? Was it one of the "in crowd" at the often socially stratified school, who might have cared for Sue Ann, but was afraid to be seen at her funeral for fear of being ostracized by friends?

Mary McGee gently nudged her husband and nodded toward the figure. Looking into the distance, Frank McGee shrugged his shoulders. No one was there. Was that lone figure a figment of Mary's imagination?

Sue Ann had been the apple of her parents' eyes, and despite the knowledge that their daughter had been pregnant, Mary and Frank McGee simply had no place in their hearts for recriminations. Many people in the town were talking about how wanton Sue Ann must have been. In fact, two paragons of virtue even noted that her death might be God's revenge for her disreputable behaviour. No doubt, these magnificent specimens of virtue had never done an ill deed in their lives. Well, except for being hypocritical that is.

Few people had ever seen Sue Ann with a boy. Her parents knew of no romantic interest on her part whatsoever. In fact, Sue Ann had categorically stated that she was having nothing to do with men until she achieved her dream of graduating from university and becoming a teacher. There were even those in the high school who whispered among themselves that she might be a lesbian, given the fact that she showed no real interest in boys.

On the way to the dark, long limousine of despair in preparation for the miserably melancholy ride back home, Mary stoically turned back for one last forlorn look at her beloved Sue Ann's grave and there was the lone cloaked figure again, standing over the graveside with bowed head, seemingly weeping uncontrollably. The figure tossed a rose into the opening, turned and scurried away.

Mary again nudged her husband, but by the time she motioned for him to look back at the grave, again the figure had disappeared into the nearby area filled with the ostentatious family crypts of the wealthy that was, no doubt, an economic statement of a country that promulgated class distinction even in death. Those who had nothing in life would have nothing in death. Ah, but religion had promised them the riches of heaven, so poverty was a small price to pay for that well-earned pie-in-the-sky reserved for believers.

A light rain began to fall upon the lap of the earth that was now being shovelled over Sue Ann's coffin. She was of humble birth and had lived a humble life. Her parents had sacrificed to bury her in finery and now melancholia would reign supreme in their lives. But there would be melancholia for others as well, because as the two men shovelled the dirt into the grave, a sudden chilly wind began to blow. A burst of thunder clamoured in the distance and reverberated throughout the dark, wet, sullen graveyard. It was as if Sue Ann McGee was proclaiming, "I shall not rest quietly."

CHAPTER 1
IT WAS SUE ANN McGEE

The quiet can be thunderously loud.
Darkness can display a flittering shroud.
Something ghastly in the corridor waits to parade.
There was about to be a ghostly cavalcade.
He saw a face of someone for whom he did not care.
She had been struck down in her seventeenth year.
He slumped beside the wall, overcome with fear.
Her forlorn sighs of misery were all he could hear.
Then, there was a translucent spectre floating about.
So frightened was he, that he could not even shout.
It was she whom he had tormented without mercy.
There, before him, was the ghost of Sue Ann McGee.

In 1954, the White Meteors football team won the state championship under a coach who would become a legend in North Carolina athletics. But that is a story for another book. That same year, the basketball team, which had gone without a winning season for some time, had a phenomenal run that put them on the cusp of winning the conference crown and getting a bid to the state championship tournament. All they had to do was defeat the Children's Home Raiders and they were in. Ah, but on the night of 17 February, with twelve hundred fans wildly cheering on the Asheboro team that was leading by 18 points at half-time, an event occurred that would lead to the development of what is called in today's society, an urban legend. However, this would not just be a legend. It would be an event that would forever cast a pall over the high school and make many residents wonder just what evil lurked about in the corridors near the gymnasium.

Team captain and leading scorer, Eric Parson, was in the locker-room exhorting his team-mates to continue their fervent play. The team gave a rousing cheer and filed out for the second half, but as they were making their way toward the entryway to the gymnasium, Eric tapped the coach on the shoulder and said, "Coach, gotta go to the washroom, be right out."

Coach Freeman, a gregarious, rotund man who looked like he could not bend over far enough to even pick up a basketball, much less have ever played the game, sternly replied, "Parson, this is a fine time to have to go to the washroom. Hurry up!"

As the team went out to prepare for the second half, Eric walked down the corridor. When he got to the locker-room door, he heard a faint noise, almost like a moan. He looked down the dark corridor toward the exit that led out to the football field and the moonlight was delicately dancing through the thick plate-glass in the door. It formed a ghost-like flickering white shadow that was flittering about near the lockers that lined the hallway. Eric, in a momentary daze, shook his head as if he was clearing the images that were playing tricks on his mind. He walked through the doorway and proceeded toward the washroom, but an uneasy feeling overwhelmed him.

Before going further, it might be useful to reflect back on the previous year at the school. Eric was not only an accomplished athlete, but he was the most handsome and one of the smartest youths in the school. He was also from one of the richest families in town. He was a member of the privileged class in and out of school, and he used it to maximum advantage.

Meanwhile, Sue Ann McGee was one of those groups of people who always seemed to be on the outside looking in. Still, in the white America of the 1950's, there was much more equality than there is today, even in high school. Although there were class distinctions in Asheboro, the children of the mill owners went to school with the children of the mill workers. The bank president's daughter sat in the classroom beside the son of the janitor in that bank. Of course that equality was reserved for whites, but the African-Americans were another story, because they were not allowed to attend school with whites. In polite words, children of colour in Asheboro were simply persona non grata at any schools in the white part of town. They had to attend their own schools, were barred from white restaurants, the movie theatres and even were expected to use separate washrooms and water fountains. Segregation was the acceptable norm in the southern states of America in spite of the U.S. Constitution that clearly stated "all men are created equal." Of course, most of the signers of the document were slaveholders; therefore, hypocrisy was as prevalent in 1776 as it is today. So, in this social climate, most students in 1950's, as a result of parental influence and the cultural norms of the south at the time, willingly accepted the separation of the races without question.

Regardless of the school, there are good and bad people. Fortunately, it seemed the good students far outnumbered the bad at the town's high school. However, that did not preclude some miscreant students from making a few poor souls lead school days in quiet desperation as a result of incessant bullying.

As alluded to previously, there was much less class stratification in those days than there is today; consequently, the bad elements were usually much more subtle. Among the students who seemed to take great delight in torturing those deemed easy targets for abuse was Eric Parson, and one individual he seemed to have particular disdain for was Sue Ann McGee. It is not necessary to go into all the abuse endured by Sue Ann at the hands or at the behest of Eric Parson, but a few examples will illustrate the depth of cruelty to which he was capable. Unfortunately, his penchant for cruelty was not just limited to Sue Ann, but was directed toward anyone he considered of inferior breeding, which included about 90% of the students.

One day, a bus bringing kids to school stopped behind a brand new Cadillac, which in 1953 was the car of choice for those who considered themselves affluent. It was parked in the spot reserved for buses, and the bus driver honked his horn as the driver of the Cadillac simply sat in the driver's seat talking heatedly to a young lady in the car with him, ignoring the fact that he was in the bus stop area. The driver looked back at the bus and gave him the favourite signal of contempt for the time, the middle finger of the right hand raised in defiance.

Finally, the bus driver, in frustration, opened the door and signalled for the children to get out. He had looked down at the licence plate of the car and realized who the driver was. It was Eric Parson.

The plate was as ostentatious as Eric was. It boldly proclaimed, "BBSTAR." It was true, Eric was a basketball star, but he was more than that. He was one of the top students academically as well, and was an all-conference end on the football team, the captain of the baseball team, the debate team captain, the student body president and his striking good looks made him the guy who made girl's hearts flutter when he merely walked by them. Well, most girls that is. There was one girl, Sue Ann McGee, who saw through his arrogance as nothing more than a mask for deep-rooted feelings of inferiority. Eric was the fourth child of Marilyn and Franklin Parson, and had three older brothers who were all successful in school, in sports and in their professional lives. As the son of the man who owned Parson Manufacturing, much was expected of Eric and, to his credit, he worked hard to live up to expectations, but could never quiet satisfy the standards set by his domineering father, who kept reminding him of how talented and successful his brothers were. No matter what Eric did, it seemed to be inadequate for his father and often his mother, who would always use his brothers as examples of what Eric should be. Yet, on the surface, no one would be aware of the turmoil that was raging within him. Of course, this is just a statement of fact for the edification of the reader, not a justification for Eric's cruelty. There are demons deep within us all, and it is easy to judge without knowing the depths of pain that so many must struggle against. Still, that cannot excuse Eric's cruelty that was directed at those who are easy targets for the arrogant, self-centered, conceited, pretentious and smug who look down upon others whom they think do not quiet measure up. The world of then, as today, seemed to cater to the privileged while ignoring the more ignoble or inferior who were deemed less worthy.

That day, as Sue Ann passed the parked car where Eric, while ignoring the sign that read *Bus Parking Only*, was talking to Mary Lou Hinton, the only daughter of the town's most prominent attorney, she realized that there were those individuals in the world who would always think that by virtue of birth and position in life, they did not have to follow the same rules as others. For some, the normal rules just did not apply. Eric Parson and Mary Lou Hinton were two of those people.

Sue Ann had seen this kind of arrogance on the part of the privileged all her life, and this day, as she was entering the school, exhausted and mentally drained after studying all night for an exam, she simply was overwhelmed with disdain for those who thought themselves above the rules that most had to obey. Looking into the car at the two, she stared at them and shook her head with audacious contempt for what she saw as unmitigated arrogance. It was an act for which she would pay dearly. Standing against the arrogance of the privileged is a deed that is rarely tolerated in a society where the few are too often exalted over the many.

Eric looked at Sue Ann with a scowl on his faced and said, "what you looking at bitch. Take a hike!"

Sue Ann, determined to finally stand up to the arrogance of those who had often made her life and the lives of others like her a living hell, refused to cower in fear. She smiled as she continued walking toward the entrance and said, "You need a dose of humility, jerk!"

Eric, livid with rage that someone from the lower strata of what he perceived as the high school social hierarchy would stand up to him, jumped out of the car, ran up in front of Sue Ann and blocked her way. "You bitch; you can't talk to me like that! Who do you think you are?"

Sue Ann, usually demure and non-combative, did not waver in her determination. "You pin-headed, self-centered, egotistical jerk, get out of my way or I'll kick you in the groin and you can spend the rest of the day trying to recover your manhood, which you don't have much of anyway."

Eric was so shocked that he just stood there as Sue Ann walked around him and up the stairs into the school. Several other students had a smile on their faces as a result of Sue Ann's bold action. For one of the few times in his life, Eric was at a loss for words.

Getting back in the car and furiously slamming the door, Mary Lou greeted him with an admonition. "Are you going to let that low class trailer trash talk to you like that and get away with it?"

Eric, determined and defiant replied, "You better believe I'm not. Just wait. I am going to figure out a way to get her, but good. I will make it my personal mission in life to make every day at this school a living hell for her. Are you with me?"

"You bet I am. It is time she learned her place, and we are the two best people to put her there. This is total, absolute war!"

So, the stage was set for a war between Eric, Mary Lou and their friends with Sue Ann McGee. Like all wars between the haves and have-nots, those at the top had all the advantages. Sue Ann would forge a strange alliance in the process, but the end result would be catastrophic.

The high school, well as it was managed, still had its share of those temptations which make school a world to train for either good or evil. The majority of the students who attended the school, despite whatever their family's social or economic status, were kind individuals with a propensity for doing the positive, rather than the negative, and did not judge people by their economic or social status. However, there was an element in the school that simply reeked of evil, a group of individuals who seemed to take particular delight in demeaning those they considered beneath them. Eric and Mary Lou were the ring leaders of this small minority of 12 to 15 students who represented the very apex of depraved, destructive loathsomeness. To that number could be added the 15 to 20 they used as their vassals of evil intentions. So, there was a total of 30 to 35 students who simply exercised no restraint in their abysmal behaviour. Up against this were the majority of the students, who were, too often, complacent in allowing those at the top to promulgate their evil unopposed.

As a group of those professing allegiance to Eric and Mary Lou gathered one morning on the steps to the school, Sue Ann McGee strode toward the doorway, and noticed they were all staring daggers at her, almost as if they could literally kill with their eyes. She did not waver, but held her head high as she walked into school.

There was a slight mist falling, and three girls standing in the group raised their umbrellas, as their eyes followed Sue Ann into the school.

"She's quite a pretty girl" said Alicia Anderson, "but of course we can have nothing to do with a low life who acts like she is something special, when we all know she is nothing but pure trailer trash. Her parents are so poor they actually moved from a trailer to a converted barn. Now, when you live in a barn like an animal, you are about as low as you can get."

Myra Lewton, bleached blond, painted-up siren of the school and the only child of Asheboro's most successful home builder, in her usual brusque manner, interjected, "You got that right. I hear her first date was with the family cow. Then she found out a cow could only be a female, so she dumped it for the family jackass. Now, she is in love!"

All present joined in raucous laughter as the bell rang and they began to saunter off in different directions to class. This was the day that would mark the beginning of an incessant attempt by a few arrogant, self-absorbed miscreants to destroy one human being who had the courage to stand up against arrogance. Like the world of today, in 1953, those who make a stand against injustice often suffer dire consequences, and Sue Ann McGee was now these people's victim of choice. What would be left of her young life would often be a living hell the next few months, but there would also be a spark that would light the candle of hope for her, only to be extinguished by a series of cataclysmic events leading to her death.

Sue Ann McGee had endured more than any child should have to endure in a country that prides itself as being the land of opportunity. In fact, opportunities for people like Sue Ann have always been limited simply because people have the misfortune of being born into poverty. The country where Sue Ann lived had a government and populace that too often looked upon poverty as a disease, rather than a condition foisted upon people who simply had no choice. Can a child pick his or her parents or the economic conditions into which they are born? Like the majority of the people in the world who have to beg for a crumb from the table of plenty set for the few, Sue Ann was a victim of birth, rather than a beneficiary. She was like so many people in a country with great promise, but too little hope. She was relegated to a lot in life proscribed by a system based on greed that let all the good things flow to those at the top of the economic ladder. Her own parents entertained little hope that their daughter would be able to climb out of the poverty that was their lot in life. Mary and Frank McGee had made the mistake of having a child when they thought there was some hope. He had a good job with a local small business that made wooden rockers. So, in 1936, they decided to have a child, but within a year, Frank was let go when a larger company bought the small firm out and decided to move the plant to Mississippi, where labour was cheaper. Frank found odd jobs, and finally got on at the ice-plant, but in 1942, he was drafted during World War II, and spent three years fighting in North Africa and Italy. Upon returning home, like all G.I.'s, he was entitled to his old job back. The only problem was people no longer were using ice-boxes. They had converted to electric refrigerators and the ice plant closed.

Since then, Frank had taken whatever work he could find to survive. He, like so many others, did not realize it, but the world was beginning a slow metamorphosis to corporate control that would make people dependent on corporations for jobs, homes, food and transportation. The old world where people could have a plot of land, grow some crops, have a few animals and provide their own sustenance was dying. It was the beginning of a society where the few would have complete freedom to exploit the many with the willing acquiescence of the government. The days of true freedom were dying fast, and the irony was that the people did not even realize what was happening to them. Even today, the people of America still believe they are free, but they do not realize that if you are dependent on a corporation for all the things you need to survive in life, you are never really emancipated or independent.

So, Sue Ann McGee was also a victim just like her mother and father, simply by virtue of birth. In a society where the privileged receive most of the benefits, the poor are nothing but an afterthought. Yet, she was determined to claw her way out of poverty. Her goal was to be a teacher like the dear Miss Bowdin, whom she admired so much.

Sue Ann was a slight, shabbily dressed young woman with a beautiful, almost glowing face. She was beautiful in the truest sense of the word; it did not at all match with the shabby, faded clothes which she wore. She had large deep-brown eyes, jet-black hair, and a sweet, fresh complexion. Her expression was bewitching, and when she smiled, a dimple appeared on her left cheek.

With her well worn satchel of books slung on her right arm, Sue Ann strolled down the hallway toward Miss Bowdin's 9:30 biology class. She looked to the right and left constantly as though she were slightly alarmed. Her manor was extremely cautious, because she sensed that something was amiss in the hallway, and then it happened. Eric Parson's best friend, Rob Waterhouse, walked up beside Sue Ann and said, "So, how's it going Sue Ann?"

Now Rob was almost as good-looking as Eric. He was tall, lean and muscular. His flowing, long, slightly curly dark brown hair hung over his ears, which for 1953, was a definite sign of a person who thought for himself, as most young boys were wearing crew cuts or that latest fad called a flat-top. Like today's youths, who are easily manipulated by popular culture, the youths of 1953 were just as readily susceptible to the manipulations of the group mentality that make most follow the crowd, rather than think for themselves. Yet, Rob, unlike the peers in his group, had something deep within him that made him realize what he was about to do was an inappropriate way to treat a person who just happened to be from a different socio-economic background than he and those whom he dutifully called friends. He even found himself wondering why he didn't refuse to go along with the prank they were about to play. It wasn't right and he knew it. Yet, he could not muster the courage to stand against their cruelty. He had an intense fear that if he took a stand it might lead to being ostracized from the group that was the very core of his existence in the high school culture that had a definite hierarchy just like the society at large. He couldn't risk losing his social standing.

Sue Ann had never been one to associate with any of that group that was euphemistically referred to by those deemed not worthy of belonging to it as "those blue-bloods." Consequently, she was taken aback at the interest Rob was showing toward her. She sensed that something was amiss. Still, she replied to his question about what's up with politeness. "Well, not much, I probably am getting ready to fail an English test. How are things with you?"

"Pretty good, Sue Ann," replied Rob. He then asked her if she wanted to have lunch with him outside on the quad. Sue Ann, still sceptical at his interest in her, could never-the-less not resist the temptation to spend time with someone who was a member of the "blue bloods," but had always been relatively cordial toward her, and she had to admit that she was attracted to him. Consequently, she graciously accepted his invitation to lunch. It would be a big mistake.

As she and Rob sat at the picnic table enjoying lunch, a dastardly deed of revenge that had been formulated by Mary Lou and Eric was about to unfold. Sue Ann was so enthralled with the attention she was receiving from Rob that she did not notice Alicia Anderson slipping up behind her. As Sue Ann and Rob continued their conversation, Alicia very calmly and quietly reached into her purse and brought out a bottle of thick red ink. She winked at Rob, which was the signal for him to get Sue Ann's attention. In order to get Sue Ann to turn toward him, Rob said, "Sue Ann, lean over here, you have a string in your hair, and I will be your knight in shining armour and remove it. I just love playing Sir Lancelot."

Sue Ann, thrilled with the attention she was receiving from a boy she had always had strong feelings for, did so as she contemplated how wonderful it would feel to have him stroke her hair. As she leaned over, Alicia quickly poured the ink into her cup of tea and slinked away unnoticed.

As Rob played at removing a nonexistent string, he had second thoughts about what was going to happen, but still he could not bring himself to take a stand against the injustice that was about to be perpetrated against Sue Ann. It was something that he would regret the rest of his life.

Sue Ann turned, and without looking into her cup, she took a drink of the tea. The ink was so coarse tasting that she gagged and spit it all over her white blouse, staining it with the ink. As she gasp for breath and coughed, a roar of laughter went up among the "blue bloods" who had all gathered at a nearby wall to observe their handiwork. The raucous laughter made Sue Ann ashamed that she had fallen for the ploy perpetrated by Rob. She had let her feelings for him interfere with the prudence needed to avert retribution by those who thought all should bow before their supposed superiority.

She got up and looked down at Rob, who now realized that his behaviour was atrocious and unbecoming of someone who prided himself on trying to be fair in most circumstances. Yet, his shame was not overwhelming enough to keep him from looking at his friends and giving them a slight grin of affirmation. He was ashamed, but not enough to risk his standing among the "blue bloods."

Sue Ann's friend, Vicky Martin, ran to escort her to the washroom, while the laughter continued unabated. Vicky, one of the few people in the school willing to stand up to the "blue bloods," said, "those jerks are going to get theirs one of these days."

Sue Ann, still gagging from the ingestion of ink, shook her head and said, "Those people never suffer retribution. They are born into privilege and they live privileged lives while most of us struggle to survive in a world that has and always will cater to those at the top. The feudal system has never died. It is still around, only it is called capitalism today."

The two girls were late to class and were admonished by the teacher, inducing laughter from the few blood bloods that were in the class, and in spite of Vicky's pleas to report the incident to the principal, Sue Ann refused, saying, "it is just my word against theirs, and theirs always counts for more because of who they are."

Days went by and Sue Ann thought the hazing was over. She assumed that Eric and Mary Lou were satisfied that they had showed her the results of any attempt to stand up to them. Unfortunately, she was mistaken. On Friday, the basketball team was set to play Thomasville. Mary Lou and Eric had arranged for what would be the pièce de résistance of revenge.

Sue Ann was in the school pep band and played at every home game; cosnequently, she was at the Friday night game, sitting in her usual spot in the stands near the player's bench with her large sousaphone blasting away.

Eric and Mary Lou had an insatiable appetite for cruelty against anyone who dared question what they considered the ordained pecking-order of the social strata that elevated a certain group of people in the high school to exalted status. Sue Ann had dared question that order, and she would suffer the consequences.

Sue Ann was on the front row at the end seat. At half time, the pep band would go out on the court and play a few numbers while doing a routine. Just as the buzzer to end the 2nd period was about to sound, in order to distract Sue Ann, Myra Lewton walked up the row of seats beside her, turned toward Sue Ann and said, "I hope you blow so hard on that big, ugly horn that your eyes pop-out."

As Myra made that comment, Sue Ann turned her head toward Myra just as Mary Lou walked in front of her and slipped a small balloon filled with the same red ink that had been used so effectively before into the opening of the tuba, while Sue Ann was sarcastically replying to Myra's comment by saying, "beauty without depth is just decoration. You are too stupid to comprehend what that means, but intellectually, you are a decoration of moronic proportions."

Accomplishing her goal of distraction, Myra, not understanding the meaning of what Sue Ann had said, simply shrugged her shoulders and proceeded up into the stands.

Sue Ann, quickly recovering her composure, got up to march with the other members of the pep band onto the court. They played "When the Saints Go Marching In" while forming a line at mid-court. Within the sousaphone, the balloon was gyrating against the sides of the tuba as Sue Ann valiantly tried to play the instrument to no avail. Soon, the balloon popped, and the liquid ran down into Sue Ann's mouth. She gagged and began spitting out the red ink in a convulsive reaction as the ink cascaded down her blouse onto the floor while the hundreds of people in the stands started laughing. Running off the court, she saw Eric standing in the doorway to the locker rooms. He smiled and threw his hands up in a disdainful gesture; smugly and arrogantly enjoying the embarrassment he had cause Sue Ann.

The vindictive pranks would continue unabated for many months, and the recourse available for Sue Ann was limited, since, at this time, there were no strict standards in regards to bullying. This type of behaviour was generally just accepted as part of the normal course of things that were part of the high school experience. Unfortunately, high school was like life in general – the vulnerable were always easy prey for those who felt themselves superior.

For the next five months, Sue Ann's life was a living hell each day she was in school, courtesy of the blue bloods. Yet, she persevered and continued to hold her head high, refusing to bow before the tyranny of those who seemed to take great delight in their evil deeds. Then, one day in gym class, Sue Ann, whose lack of athletic ability, seemed to always make Miss Fields eager to embarrass her by making her first to perform any task, signalled that the first one up the grappling rope would be Sue Ann. Thus, Sue Ann, determined to show Miss Fields and the blue bloods in class that she was capable of performing athletically, doggedly scurried up the rope, all the way to the top. When she got there, she looked up toward top of the ceiling where the rope was wrapped around a beam and a look of horror came over her. She was doomed, her life was finished. Seeing the flayed end of the rope, she could not even scream. All she did was accept her fate as she plunged toward the floor. Thus would end the pranks played on Sue Ann. But the pranks would come back to haunt Eric later in the corridor outside the locker room. What occurred that night would remind everyone that the dead do not always rest quietly.

We now return to Eric, as he exited the locker room that faithful night months later. The darkness of the hallway was so thick you could seemingly cut it with a knife. It wasn't just the darkness, it was a feeling. And the cold seemed to cut though to the bone. Eric stood there, shivering, unable to move down the hallway toward the entrance to the court. His feet seemed to be encased in concrete. His heart raced frantically as he fought to avoid looking behind him, but he could not help himself. It was almost as if some unseen strong hand was forcing him to turn his head and look back down the corridor. He finally could resist no longer, as he slowly but determinedly turned his head. Flittering about in the darkness at the end of the corridor was a ghostly figure, slowly moving his way, seeming to float menacingly toward him. His chest heaved up and down frantically as the vision began to come into focus, rising from the darkness, and it looked into his eyes, which were full of fear. Eric's pupils grew to the size of quarters as the face slowly became visible. Oh no, oh no, it was Sue Ann McGee.

. CHAPTER 2
FACE THE WRATH OF SUE ANN McGEE

I come back to let you know
that though I am dead,
I am not at peace.
I long for justice.
It was a senseless death.
How senseless and cruel.
But when I realized the truth,
it was too late ... too late.
I shall not rest
until the truth be known.

Eric, screaming and running toward the entryway just as the second half was about to start, caused such a commotion that the crowd and the players who were filing onto the court stood in amazement at his frantic dash for the safety of the gym. The lights in the gym began to flicker and suddenly went completely out. Then, as Eric came to an abrupt halt at the team bench, frantically shouting, "it's Sue Ann, it is Sue Ann," a loud moan rumbled throughout the gym, seemingly making the walls vibrate. There was a holler, a whine and a cry. The voice was thin and the moan was high and from the entryway came a crackling, howling wind that seemed to bring terror all through the gym. The light of the moon was filtering in through the skylights, flickering all about. Then, as the crowd looked toward the place from whence the sounds came, the lights came on, but the corridor was still deathly dark. There, near the entryway, was a sight that brought collective terror to those assembled that night.

Ah, it was as if Edgar Allen Poe had conjured up one of his literary spirits to haunt those in the gym that night. All eyes seemed to stare toward the corridor from which Eric had fled, and there about ten feet into the darkness a spectre danced as if trapped in excruciating pain, moaning sorrowfully. Its long dark hair was flowing all about, and the white dress upon it formed a bright glow. Then it turned and the back of the white dress was bare. Yes, it was as if part of it was missing. The spectre fluttered down the hallway, slowly dissipating as the crowd scurried in fear toward the exits as the lights went out again, plunging the gym into darkness. All the while, Eric kept shouting, "Sue Ann. I tell you; it is Sue Ann."

The game was called, and the effect would be devastating for the team, as they seemed to never recover from that night, losing every game afterward, tumbling from first place all the way to last. The local newspaper covered what it termed an obvious prank played by the Thomasville team when they saw they were about to lose the game. Yet, no evidence of such a prank was ever found, and at each home game, the crowd seemed to be more interested in keeping an eye on the corridor than the game. However, no disturbance occurred.

Through all this time, Eric insisted to his friends that he had indeed encountered the ghost of Sue Ann McGee, but they all scoffed at him. Yet, he steadfastly refused to go into the corridor alone. In fact, not only did it affect his play to the point that the coach eventually benched him, but his grades became so abysmal that his parents hired private tutors to assure that he would still be able to graduate and attend Duke University.

Over time, the events of that evening began to fade from people' minds, but among the students, there were still whispers about what went on that night and many students stayed extremely weary of the corridor, few willing to venture down it alone, even in the daytime. There was also an intense cold in the corridor, and no amount of heat seemed to alleviate the situation. Then, on graduation night the 4th of June 1954, as a throng of people gathered to watch the ceremony at the football stadium that was adjacent to the high school, the 125 graduates, for convenience, gathered in the gymnasium and were preparing to walk down the dreaded corridor where Eric said he had seen the ghost of Sue Ann McGee, proceed out the exit at the end of the hall and walk to the stadium. Eric felt great trepidation, but he was determined to walk down the corridor with his classmates unafraid. What happened next has been oft debated by those who were there, and, no doubt, embellished over the years by those who told and retold the story. It is not our purpose here to question the authenticity of what is about to be shared, but rather to state it comes from an authoritative source who was in the corridor that night.

As the students made their way down the corridor, the lights began to fade and flickering shadows along the varnished walls danced about. There was an intense feeling of melancholia that permeated the hot, humid June air. Then, a low moan rumbled from the floor like a lonely creature pleading from the pits of hell to be released from agony. It was as if something or someone was begging for solace from those enjoying life. The moaning voice appeared to be pleading for help in dealing with the pain of deep, dark, lonely death.

As the students scurried toward the door, anxious to escape to the safety of the crowd, the door would not open. Miss Fields, who was leading the procession, started to frantically ask some of the bigger boys to push it open, but as they furiously banged their shoulders into it, the door would not budge. Suddenly there was an intense banging noise, as if someone was pounding on the walls, the ceiling and the floor. All this time, the moaning continued, reverberating off the walls and echoing down the hallway. Panic was beginning to sit in. Some students turned and ran toward the gym entryway, but as they got there, the giant steel doors slammed shut, preventing them from escaping into the gym. A few of them, putting their hands over their ears to drown out the pounding and the moaning, sit down on the floor. Many were weeping and others were beginning to scream.

Eric Parson, who had already experienced one monumental frightening night in the corridor, was leaning against the wall, and began to slowly edge downward until he was sitting on the floor with his knees up to his chin, which he rested on them as he hid his face. He was breathing heavily, overwhelmed with fear. It was then that he felt the light touch of a girl's hand on his left shoulder. He turned and looked up. There she was, and this time several other students saw her. Yes, the faint white outline, the haggard and drawn face was that of Sue Ann McGee. Suddenly, mass hysteria abounded as screaming filled the corridor and the overhead light bulbs flickered on as the ghostly figure dissipated into nothingness. Eric sat in horror, just staring into the spot where he had seen Sue Ann. The lights began to pop and the glass fell onto the students, cutting and burning them.

By this time, the screams had been heard outside and several parents were desperately trying to get the outside door open. Another group of people had entered the gymnasium from the other side of the building and were attempting to get the entryway doors open. All the time, the frenzied students were screaming in fear as a small fire started to burn on the ceiling around the light fixtures. The toxic fumes from the popping light bulbs caused burning eyes and intense coughing. The moans and the pounding were all replaced with the sounds of frenzied fear as it became apparent that 125 people were trapped in a corridor of death.

One man removed the fire axe from the gym wall, hit the fire alarm and began to furiously hack at the steel doors. It was all to no avail. The corridor was filling with smoke. Then, there was a cold breeze that blew through the corridor, seemingly coming from nowhere. It swirled about, putting out the flames on the ceiling, and finally, the man hacking at the steel door broke through and the doors swung open. The students rushed from the horror to the outside where they were hugged by their terrified parents. Eric Parson was the last one to leave the corridor, pulled up from his sitting position by Miss Fields who said something strange. "Don't worry Eric, I know all about it, but it will never be revealed. I am on your side."

Extensive repairs had to be done to the corridor and workmen were scraping the ceiling one day, prepping it for skimming with stucco. Two men were on a scaffold, as their helper waited below. They hollered down for a bucket of water. The man left and went into the locker room to get some water out of the shower.

As the man stepped out of the locker room into the hallway, there was a pale-looking young girl with dark, sorrowful eyes standing there in a beautiful white dress. Shocked at seeing her, since the door to the gym was locked, he said, "You can't be in here. It's dangerous."

She did not say a word, just smiled, turned and walked toward the entryway to the gym. At that instance the two men were hollering, "get the water down here, hurry!" The man turned and started walking toward the scaffold, then looked back over his shoulder. The young girl was gone, seemingly disappearing in an instance. Where was she? She did not have time to get through the gym and out the door.

The two men on the scaffold looked down and asked what took so long. The reply was, "there was a girl up there. Did you see her?"

Looking up at the entryway to the gym, the two men on the scaffold got looks of horror on their faces, and the one below knew something was frightening them, so he turned and looked in the direction their gazes were focused. There, in the entryway was a sight that brought cold chills to all three men. Seeming to float about, just inside the corridor, was a girl in white. She had a translucent form; prominent, piercing, resolute brown eyes that seemed to be pleading for solace and rest from pain; and thick, coal-black hair that cascaded down over her shoulders as it fluttered from a nonexistent breeze. Her expression conveyed great pain and agony, and she emitted a pitiful, mournful cry that echoed off the corridor walls and penetrated to the very core of each man's soul.

The two men on the scaffold scurried down so hurriedly that they both plummeted onto the floor and the cracking of bones could be heard above the pitiful cries of the spectre before them. Running toward the back exit, the uninjured worker pounded furiously on the exit door, trying unsuccessfully to get it open as the two men on the floor, unable to move from the excruciating pain of their injuries cowered in fear as the translucent apparition moved slowly down the hall, whining as if suffering intolerable agony. It was almost as if the spectre was pleading for something, but for what? About half way down the hall, the spectre floated toward the ceiling 25 feet above and disappeared.

The three men told their story to all who would listen, but laughter was the general response, followed by the admonition, "you guys need to lay off the booze during the day. It's giving you hallucinations." Still, three days later, a similar incident occurred when three other men continued the work. Only this time, the spectre disappeared into a locker in the hallway. Those three men refused to go back again. Finally, the contractor found three men who scoffed at tales of a ghost that was now spreading throughout the school and the town. However, their scepticism was short-lived.

As the workers were preparing to leave around 4:00 PM, the sky became exceedingly cloudy and lightning could be seen off in the distance. The rumble of thunder was faint, but the muffled sound seemed to portend a coming calamity as the sky got blacker and blacker while the workers were loading material onto their truck. Walking through the entryway into the corridor to pick up the last of their supplies, the three of them noticed an even more intense cold that was not there before. They looked at one another quizzically, but continued down the hallway, picked up the last of their materials and turned to leave. There, in the entryway, was a young girl dressed in white, striding their way. She was forlorn looking and seemed to be in a daze. She turned to her right when she got to the locker room door, opened the door and went in. The men, concerned that they would lock her in the gym went into the locker room to look for her, but the search was in vain. She had simply disappeared. They even opened every locker in the room, stood and stared at one another in disbelief as one of them said, "Strangest thing I have ever seen. Where could she have gone?" Then he pointed toward the door, as he continued, "that is the only door in or out. She looked almost ghost-like. I am beginning to believe in ghosts."

Another worker interjected, "I'm glad we are through with this job. Frankly, the intense chill in the corridor was a bit unnerving to say the least and now this. There is definitely something strange about this place. If I was the principal, I'd seal this damn corridor up and never open it again."

It would take one other occurrence many months later for the principal to do that, but it was one that would leave a more deathly legacy than the incident experienced by the men who were often mocked for their belief in a ghostly encounter. It would be an incident that would be long remembered, but unfortunately for some, not remembered long enough, because the stage was now set for the beginning of what would ultimately be a growing legacy of fear, but those who should have feared the most had already graduated on that faithful night the previous summer. They thought they were free of Sue Ann McGee when she had been laid to rest in the cemetery, but they were all sorely mistaken. Death simply was not always the end. Sue Ann McGee would prove that.

In December of 1954, before the Christmas break, a party was planned for the gymnasium on the Friday prior to the holidays. At that party, a senior named Harry Delvin was determined to make a sophomore, Ellen Stutts, submit to his romantic advances. Ellen was a 15 year old beauty who turned the heads of all the boys, and probably even some girls. She was incredibly tall for a girl at 6 feet, with shimmering, long, natural platinum blond hair that seemed to beckon for caresses. Her lips were thick and luscious. Her smile was coy and enticing. In her heart was a most precious dream to be loved by a handsome young man like Harry Devlin. She longed to be swept up into a swirling torrent of romance, so it was no surprise when she agreed to attend the Christmas party with him. After all, now that Eric Parson had graduated, he was the most popular and handsomest boy in the school.

For most of the year, there had been periodic rumblings among the students and faculty about how the corridor was always so bitterly cold, regardless of how high the heat was turned up. Still, the rumours about a ghost had pretty much been ignored by most. Yet, there were those who simply would never venture down the corridor alone. Harry and Ellen were not among those with fear or trepidation in regards to the corridor, but that was all going to change on the night of the dance. Outside, a light snow was falling as the students filed into the gym for the festivities. Their mood was gay and celebratory. It would not be that way for long.

As the DJ played Bill Haley and the Comets tunes and the students danced wildly to the beat of the music with their gyrating motions, often termed by adults of the day as representative of the devil, Harry Devlin was whispering softly in Ellen Stutt's ear, "come on Ellen, let's go down the infamous corridor and slip into the locker room for a little kiss or two. You know I have waited a long time for that first kiss. How about it?"

Ellen sheepishly grinned and said, "Promise to be a good boy?"

"I am as good as they get little girl," replied an exuberant Harry.

Unbeknownst to Ellen, Harry had made a bet with three other boys, Bob Wingate, Lou Simpson and Don Lucas that he would not only get to first base with Ellen, but hit a home run. It seems Ellen was known as what the boys termed a classic tease, and this night, Harry was going to show the three boys what a masterful manipulator of women he was. Then, when he had hit his "home run," the three other boys would blackmail her into giving them a turn. Thus, they would make the biggest tease in Asheboro, as the teens of the time said, "Go all the way." Unfortunately for the four boys, there was one calculation that they had not included in the equation. This despicable act was going to occur in the one area where it was not wise to tempt fate. This night would produce the most dramatic and deadly results yet.

Looking around to make sure that there was no one to notice them, Harry and Ellen slipped off into the corridor and down to the locker room. Harry quietly opened the door and they slipped in, where unbeknownst to Ellen, the three other boys were concealing themselves in the shower stalls. They fought back giggles as they listened to Harry attempt to work his craftiness on an unsuspecting Ellen.

At this point, it might be appropriate to interject a note on the real Ellen Stutts, because her reputation was not deserved. It had been the result of a rumour started by a former boyfriend who became frustrated with her refusal to allow him the privileges to which far too many boys think they are entitled. Upset with her, he embellished stories of how she was a tease, when in truth; she was just a young lady who thought that she was too young to make that first foray into sexual intimacy. Her steadfast refusal to submit to the young man's carnal instincts had made him so angry that he set out to destroy her reputation, which he had done a pretty good job of over the school year. So this night was a result of unfounded rumours started by a disgruntled suitor, but Ellen, through her desire to snare the affection of Harry Devlin, had put herself in an untenable situation which she would regret the rest of her life.

As the two of them kissed passionately near locker 23, which ironically had been the locker used by none other than the former number one Lothario of the school, Eric

Parson, Harry's hands began to roam into areas that Ellen had always made off limits to boys. Despite her being enamoured with Harry, she was not about to allow him to engage in the liberties he was seeking. It was at this point that Harry blurted out, "What's wrong with you, Ellen. It is time you stopped teasing and did the deed. And you are lucky it is going to be with me."

Ellen, now becoming flabbergasted with Harry replied, "I'm outta here, Harry."

Then, Harry's three friends burst forth and Bob Wingate said, "We'll tell everyone you were in here with all four of us. The whole school will be calling you a slut by the time we finish with you, so you better give us all what we want or else. And if you scream, we will bash your head in, bitch. You got it!"

As Bob, Lou and Don moved toward her, Harry smiled, and placed his hands on Ellen's shoulders, shoving her back against locker 23. He said, "we aren't going to take no for an answer, Ellen. You better realize that right now."

Ellen, her heart racing and fear overwhelming her, stood in disbelief that she had put herself in a situation that was the result of her infatuation with Harry. Now, she was going to have to pay the piper for her miscalculations of Harry's intentions. Just as she was about to scream, Lou Simpson place his hands over her mouth and started to nibble on her ear. From the other side, Don Lucas starting whispering in her other ear, "you want this and you know you do."

Harry kept her shoulder tightly pinned against the locker as Bob Wingate menacingly strutted about like a peacock, seemingly immensely proud of what they were about to do. It was then that Harry uttered something that would stir the very soul of a spirit seemingly irrevocably trapped in the eternity of the grave. In a mean-spirited, cold-hearted manner, he said, "this is going to be the most fun since Sue Ann McGee fell from the grappling rope and broke her neck. She was a bitch who liked to tease, too."

Suddenly, from behind Ellen, locker 23 began to shake, and a pounding noise in it startled the four boys so badly that Ellen was able to break herself free, but she stumbled over Harry's foot and onto the floor as she tried to run. She turned over on her back, so afraid that she could not muster the strength to arise. It was then that she saw a vapour begin to ooze out between the air slats in the locker; slowly forming the outline of what appeared to be a woman. The boys, overwhelmed with fear, ran for the door, but it would not open. They pounded on it in desperation and started screaming for help as the spectre began to take a more solid form. Yes, it was a young woman dressed in white. She had long, flowing black hair that seemed to flutter all about. Then, there came a low, mournful cry of desperation.

As the boys pounded on the door and screamed for help, Ellen lay on the floor, watching the transparent spectre move swiftly toward the boys, who were almost in shock from fright. Meanwhile, people were forming in the corridor and trying to get the door to the locker room open, but it was a futile effort.

The four boys on the inside turned their backs to the door as the spectre hovered over them menacingly, almost as if preparing for an onslaught of mischief that would wreck a frightful carnage upon those who had attempted the defilement of Ellen Stutts. The boys appeared to be on the verge of dropping to their knees and begging for mercy. Were they actually seeing a ghost-like figure or was it merely a dancing fog that had somehow taken on the form of a young girl. There was no overt action to harm them, only a fluttering spectre that was now beginning to moan with a melodic melancholia that could even be heard through the thick steel door to the corridor. In the hallway, as they were trying to get the door open, the gathering crowd looked in astonishment at one another as the moaning became so intense that it seemed to bounce off the walls and reverberate up and down the corridor.

Meanwhile, inside the locker room, Ellen had struggled to a sitting position and looked in amazement at the four boys who were cowering in fear before the fluttering spectre. Knowing they could not open the door, all four mustered the courage to run toward the showers, trying to escape the now bouncing spectre that seemed to hover menacingly above them as it was gyrating all about. Ellen moved toward the door, turned the knob, and for her, it opened. As she stepped outside to the frantic crowd, several embraced her, pulling her toward the gym entryway, asking what happened. As they were doing so, a few of the people in the corridor edged toward the door and in the shower area they heard frightful screams emitting from behind a tiled wall. Cautiously moving toward the shower area, they suddenly heard a pitiful moan that seemed to be a pleading cry for help. Then complete silence and only the whimpering sounds of the boys.

Walking into the shower area, the scene shocked and dismayed all who observed the carnage of death before them. Sitting with his back against the wall in one corner was Bob Wingate, whimpering like a child as his head bobbed up and down uncontrollably and his eyes were glassed over with fear. Lou Simpson was sprawled face down on the shower floor, his entire body convulsing from shock. Don Lucas was laying face up, his eyes transfixed on the ceiling in a death stare as a result of seeing something that had literally scared the life out of him.

Then, there was the self-styled ladies man, Harry Devlin. How does one adequately describe the damaged head that seemed to have been battered against the wall with such brute force that fragments of bone and brain matter had splattered against the white tile as the crimson blood trickled down into a puddle at the top of Harry's skull that lay open, exposing the brain? He was dead, sprawled out on the floor, but the brain's impulses had sent a final signal to his legs through frayed nerves that made his legs twitch one last time. Those standing there jumped with fright as his legs twitched. They looked all about and saw nothing but the horror of death and the shock of the two who had survived, but were still lost in the throes of horror that would forever silence them as they spent the rest of their lives in mental institutions where no one could ever reach into the depths their shattered minds.

Ah, and then there was Ellen Stutts. When asked about what happened, she steadfastly maintained that she had been unconscious though the whole ordeal. All she knew was that the four boys had tried to rape her, and apparently one of them had a change of heart and wrecked havoc on the others. She harboured the secret of what she saw that night, not out of fear, but out of gratefulness for whatever had spared her the indignities to which those four boys had tried to subject her. Ghost, demon, chivalrous spectre, whatever it was, it had saved her. It would be almost ten years before she would reveal to an intrepid investigator what really happened that night. Still, the rumours began to swell and Sue Ann McGee's name was never mentioned out loud, only whispered, as if saying it out loud might actually conjure her up again to cause mayhem. One skilful wordsmith actually sprayed on the door to the locker room in red paint: *Enter here and face the wrath of Sue Ann McGee.*

CHAPTER 3
THAT WHICH ABIDES IN THE WIND

Do not whisper to the wind,
For a spectre is waiting there.
With anxious sighs and open ears,
Just listening to the sullen air.
Waiting for someone who cares,
To answer and become aware.

Do not whisper to the wind,
For a spectre comes leather skinned,
With eyes aglow in sickly hue,
A floating figure tall and thinned.
You may not, shall not, can not
Ever whisper to the wind!

After that horrendous night, Bob Wingate was committed to a mental institution in Butner, North Carolina. He would never be in his right mind again, seemingly trapped forever by the dark horror that had invaded his mind. His voice was forever silenced and he spent the next 44 years simply staring off into space. Only occasionally, he would break out in violent twitching and blood curdling screaming as he rolled about on the floor.

Lou Simpson was taken to the hospital, where he was treated for intense shock, then transferred to the mental ward. He, like Bob, was unable to speak. After a brief sojourn in the psychiatric ward, it was finally determined that it would be best for him to return home, where, over time, his mind might actually restore itself in familiar surroundings. Unfortunately, it did not work.

On the first anniversary of the terrible incident, Lou slipped out of his house, went to the high school and broke into the gym. The corridor and locker room had been framed in with two by fours and covered with panelling. He apparently had no intention of going into the corridor, anyway. He went to the very spot where Sue Ann McGee had fallen from the grappling rope. He apparently climbed up the rope as far as he could. Then, he let go and crashed to the floor, like Sue Ann, breaking his neck. When he was found by Miss Fields the following morning, he was sprawled on the floor with a smile on his face, almost as he was relieved to be set free of the horror that had destroyed his mind.

Many years passed with no more major incidents. The sealed up area had simply been ignored for years by the students; although, sometimes when the students were in P.E. class, noises could be heard behind the wall. The normal response was, "must be rats rooting around in there." Then, in late October of 1962, the decision was made to tear down the wall and open up the corridor, so that the bands coming to perform in a battle of the bands concert planned at the football stadium could use the two locker rooms for getting dressed and simply go out the back door into the stadium. The back door had never been sealed up, but no one had gone into the corridor from the outside either. When the janitor was told to unlock the door, go in, and start cleaning it out while the carpenters were tearing down the wall, his response to the principal was, "you sure you want to do this Mr. Turkian?"

Mr. Turkian, who was not principal when the incidents occurred, tersely replied, "I know the history of the place,

Robert. However, I do not believe in ghosts. Let's put that silliness behind us and get to work."

Robert Hoover had been at the school nearly 30 years, and he had learned long ago not to defy the principal. After all, this was the south, and there were few unions to protect people from the wrath of their supervisors and employers. Unfortunately, America had always fought against unions, because they represented, according to the government, the evil of socialism. The people of America, particularly in the south, had been propagandized into seeing anything that promoted equality of opportunity as evil. The working men and women, without realizing it, were actually lining up for their invisible chains that would forever lock them into service to those at the top of the economic ladder. Robert was a man who understood that, but he, like most of the poor, simply had no power to change things. All power rested with those at the top, and only for a brief moment in the late 1960's would it look like things might actually change. It was a short-lived opportunity that fell into the deep, dark abyss of greed led by conniving corporations, hypocritical religious institutions and an uncaring government.

Robert Hoover simply bowed his head and said, "Yes sir!" However, he still felt a great uneasiness. It had been nine years since the last incident, and over the next couple of days, as he was cleaning; he always entered the corridor and locker room with great trepidation. The coldness that seemed to permeate the corridor and locker room was not normal for September in North Carolina, and he wore a sweater most days. However, the coldness would wind up being the least of his worries.

Robert was more than a janitor. He was a confidant to the students, most of whom saw him as a person who, though of humble background and means, was always there to lend assistance to those in need. In the USA, social programmes rarely provide adequately for those who are on the fringes of poverty. Even those trapped in depths of poverty are treated as if it was a disease of their own making, rather than a condition that was allowed to fester and grow, because those at the top received all the benefits while nothing but a meatless bone was thrown to those begging for sustenance. Many times Robert had shared his lunch with students whose parents struggled to put food on their tables and had to send their children off to school without a packed lunch or the money to buy food. This was a country that spent lavishly on weapons to kill people, but could not find the money to feed its hungry. It was a country that made health care a privilege rather than a right, letting people die on the hospital steps because they did not have the money to pay for care. It was a country that had rather give tax breaks to the wealthy than fund educations for those who thirsted for knowledge. This state of affairs appalled Robert. He often had his wife make extra sandwiches to share with groups of students whom he knew had parents of meagre means. He was a man of compassion, who had befriended Sue Ann McGee many years before. In her, he saw a depth of character that seemed to transcend all the students he had ever known, and her death was devastating for him. He had stood behind the coal fired furnace and cried like a baby when he heard of her death, because she had touched his heart. At her funeral, standing with Miss Bowdin, he had said to her, "that coffin is the end of great promise that will be unfulfilled now."

It was particularly hurtful to him that so many people had turned the mayhem in the corridor and locker room into an excuse to malign someone he held in high regard. He did not believe in ghosts, but he did know there was something strange about the corridor, something he simply could not understand. He was not a religious man, and in 1962 this was a bit unusual for Americans, especially in the south, where religion held an inordinate sway over the people. Still, Robert Hoover felt that, regardless of his lack of belief in God, there were things in the world that simply defied explanation. Evil, on the other hand, he did believe in, but he always found himself, after the last incident where the rape of Ellen Stutts was prevented, seeing what occurred that night as good for one person. After all, what happened to those boys actually saved Ellen Stout from evil.

In his usual meticulous manner, one day Robert was on his knees frantically cleaning the floor. On the wall above was a large shelf with metal braces. On the shelves were various items that had been deposited over the years. One item right above his head was setting precariously over the edge of the shelf. It was a large compressor for an air conditioning unit that had been in the locker room lounge. Its weight was at least 50 kilos (about 110 pounds), and all the years it had been there had put so much pressure on the shelf that the screws and brackets that attached it to the wall were loosened.

Robert was so engrossed in his intense scrubbing of filth on the floor that he did not hear the creaking of the shelf above his head. He was totally unaware that death was hovering over him.

As the shelf was about to completely collapse and send the compressor hurling down onto his head, Robert felt two unseen hands push with mighty force and send him sprawling across the floor. As he lay on his back, looking back to see what mysterious force had propelled him across the floor, the shelf collapsed, sending the compressor smashing onto the floor where he had been kneeling. A flittering mist, forming an outline of what appeared to be the blurry figure of a young woman arose from the debris and dissipated instantly. Breathing heavily, Robert continued to lay there, his mind unable to comprehend what had just occurred. Had the ghost of Sue Ann McGee saved him from certain death with a well-timed push to safety?

In the fall of 1962, Aaron Adams was preparing for his last year of high school. How does one adequately describe an adolescent Aaron? To say he was a complicated mixture of both hope and despair would be an understatement. On the outside, he appeared to be a happy-go-lucky, devil-may-care kind of guy who was always quick with witticisms and willing to reach out with the hand of compassion to those who were often ostracized by the social pecking order that, unfortunately, made high school reflective of a society that was stratified by sexual orientation, economic and social status. Although from a relatively affluent family, as a result of an entrepreneurial father who was a successful businessman, Aaron was certainly not part of the country club set, as his father was uneducated and came from a working-class background. Underneath, there was that inner turmoil in Aaron that is so common to children who must endure the agony of an alcoholic parent. Although

Aaron's father was not physically abusive, his alcoholism did often lead to psychological abuse from a father who often seemed disappointed in a son who didn't quiet measure up to what his father expected of him. Yet, father and son had a great deal of simpatico when it came to disdain for those who thought that their education or wealth should garner them more respect. On religion, they both abhorred the fear that it used to keep people in line, and to trap them into abiding by a set of rules that they both saw as inhibiting the real compassion that humans should show for one another. Although his father was uneducated, Aaron would always look upon him as the smartest man he had ever known. It was his father who taught him that being educated did not necessarily mean you were smart. As his father always said, "the world is full of educated fools." Likewise, his father told him in regards to religion, "it is easy to condemn people, but it is hard to reach out with compassion to them. Religion too often puts condemnation before compassion. That is why, when a man says he is a Christian, I put my hand on my wallet, because God always needs money. He doesn't pay taxes. He has magnificent churches. This being is supposed to be all-knowing, all-wise, completely perfect, but he is always in need of money. People with God on their side should always be suspect, because the God I have read about was a pretty cruel person. Allowing a father to sell his daughter to the highest bidder, asking a father to sacrifice his son, telling a parent they can kill a rebellious son, sending plagues to destroy innocent children is just not my idea of love. Think about it. Religion has actually convinced people that there's an invisible man living in the sky who watches everything you do, every minute of every day. And the invisible man has a list of ten things he does not want you to do. And if you do any of these things, he has a special place, full of blazing fires and smoke, torture, misery and anguish, where he will send sinners to suffer for eternity. Yet, he loves you. Frankly son that is not the kind of love I would expect from God." Then, the two of them would share joyous laughter, and Aaron would feel a sense of deep respect for his father, who had no religion, but truly knew the meaning of compassion by being a man who tried to help those in need.

Of course, the use of fear to keep the American people in line was as prevalent then as it is today. Although it was not the Muslims the American people were propagandized into fearing, but the Russians (Soviets). The U.S. government constantly promoted fear of any country that was not capitalistic, particularly communist Russia and China.

So fearful were the people of an immanent nuclear attack by the Soviets that many families spent thousands of dollars building fall-out shelters deep in the ground, where they would supposedly spend years waiting for the fall-out to disappear. Then, they would emerge from the depths of the earth and start rebuilding a capitalist society that had triumphed over the evil of communism.

This constant bombardment of the populace with propaganda about an impending strike by an "evil empire" kept, not only adults on edge, but made children of all ages live in constant fear of death from the skies. Children, at the start of every school day, stood ramrod straight and dutifully recited the Pledge of Allegiance:

White Meteors and the Ghost of Sue Ann McGee

I pledge allegiance to the flag of the United States of America, and to the republic for which it stands, one nation under God, indivisible, with liberty and justice for all.

Aaron often reflected on that statement, especially the part about liberty and justice for all; because he had African-American friends who were forced to live in the area of the town know as "Nigger Hill." Nor were the children from the African American community allowed to attend the all white, new high school. Rather, they were forced to go to school in an old, dilapidated building. He would always reflect as he was forced to recite the Pledge on just how much freedom and liberty his black friend, Colon Loudon, had in a country that sanctioned segregation in the southern states. And then there was that part about God. Even at the age of 17, Aaron was an agnostic, because he had a father who taught him to question everything, rather than just accept whatever was said as truth. Still, Aaron dutifully stood and recited those words, even listening to a morning devotional over the public address system that always ended with a prayer and the words, "in Jesus' name, we pray." He wondered what his Jewish friend, Yergin Bernstein, thought about being forced to listen to a prayer intended for an entity that was foreign to his religion. Those kinds of anomalies made Aaron wonder just how much freedom the American people really had. Was it more an illusion than reality?

Aaron's father had always told him that any man who relied on others to put food on his table was a slave. To his father, the only truly free people were those who could grow their own food, hunt game in the forest, make their own clothes and have shelter they built themselves. Aaron's father did none of those things, but if he had to do so, he could return to those days of his youth when his own father and mother provided for the family that way. Aaron actually felt he was a victim of an era where the individual was rapidly losing control of his own destiny; in a sense, being forced into a situation that made everyone dependent, rather than independent. It was simply the way of the modern world that had been turned over for exploitation by the corporations.

Aaron was tall, lean and frankly a bit awkward looking. Still, he did not let his looks keep him from pursuing the ladies. He always followed his father's advice about women: "son, ask ten women to go out with you, and nine might say no, but when the one says yes, you forget about the nine who said no." Therefore, Aaron was not shy about asking for dates, and he got a lot of no's, but when he got the yes's, he realized his father was right.

One girl who had been telling Aaron "no" since grammar school was the school heartthrob, Casey Felton. Her shimmering, long brown hair that cascaded over her shoulders, gorgeous heart-shaped face, irresistible luminous dark brown eyes, wide mouth with pouty kissable lips, adorable dimples, brilliant white teeth, naughty expression and long fluttering eyelashes made Aaron's heart race every time he got near her.

Since the second grade, Aaron had longed to just reach down and hold her hand once, but alas, she was always out of his reach. Although not dismissive of him, she simply had no romantic inclinations toward Aaron. Every school dance, every class they shared, every time he saw her in the lunchroom, every time he saw her gracefully and sensuously stroll down the hall, Aaron's heart raced like a raging river through a gorge. He had not asked her for a date since the 10th grade, when she told him, "Aaron, you are a nice boy, but I simply have no interest in going on a date with you. Please, if you want to continue to be friends, don't ask me again." So, it had been over two years since she had issued her final "no." However, things were about to change for the both of them in January of 1963, when they returned from Christmas vacation.

By this time, the locker room and hallway had been reopened for over two months, and there had been no incidents whatsoever, other than what happened to Robert Hoover, who had told no one about it. However, the cold in the corridor was still there for all to observe, but the tales of Sue Ann McGee had faded into obscurity, with few students ever bringing up the stories about spectres appearing in the hallway and the locker room deaths many years before. Still, there seemed to be some trepidation on the part of most students when they ventured down the hallway or into the locker room. In fact, most students avoided the area if at all possible. There was just something foreboding about it. It was almost as if there was an unwritten rule to not talk about all the strange occurrences there; consequently, perhaps there would be nothing to fear.

There are two types of fear. The first is environmental and poses a direct physical threat to the perceiver. The second is strictly psychological and poses no direct physical threat. For obvious reasons the first is a rational fear and the second is irrational.

Rational fears can be overcome by physical retaliation or escape, whereas irrational fears play upon the psyche and can be successfully overcome only by conscious and rational control. Aaron Adams was a young man who simply had no fears. He did not believe in ghosts, nor did he have any religious beliefs that perpetrated the ideas of demons and devils lurking about to cause mischief. For years, he had heard the tales of Sue Ann McGee's ghost haunting the area behind the gym, but he laughed them off as just mere tall tales from those who could not think rationally. The deaths that had occurred there and the eerie sightings of a spectre had logical explanations, even if no one had come up with them yet. Aaron's mind was simply not open to accepting the supernatural, whether it dealt with God, angels or ghostly spectres floating about in the hallway and locker room. It was all ridiculous to him.

Casey Felton, like Aaron, was a bit of an anomaly at the time. Although she was definitely one of the "in crowd," she was not your typical teenage girl of the 1960's who dreamed of being swept up in the arms of the captain of the football team or getting picked as homecoming queen. In fact, like Aaron, she did not drink alcohol, rarely used profanity, was not concerned with impressing anyone and was more interested in the plight of the underprivileged in a country with vast wealth and the ability to eradicate poverty than she was with the latest Hollywood gossip, television shows, bands or fashion trends. Although most of her close friends came from the upper echelon of the high school pecking order, she was always sociable and cordial with everyone, and was respected for her kindness and politeness by all.

Sue Ann McGee was a distant memory for all the students at the high school, but an event in late January of 1963 would make two inquisitive students seek out details on her violent death that had been overlooked for almost ten long years. Those two students, Aaron and Casey, were about to light a fuse that would blow the lid off a dark secret.

Sue Ann's chief nemesis, Eric Parson, had gone to Duke University after high school. Then he attended law school at the University of North Carolina. Although not in private practice, he was handling all legal matters for Parson manufacturing, where he worked with his father and brothers. At the end of every January, the high school had what was referred to as career day, where local business people and skilled trades' people came in to offer career advice to students who were interested in certain occupations.

The military, which needed fresh recruits for the growing war in Vietnam, was always invited to extol patriot service to the primarily lower-class students who could not afford university and were excellent recruits to be cannon fodder in unnecessary wars while the upper-class students were given a pass on patriotism. This is mentioned, because at this particular career day, Casey and Aaron were members of a small group of students who had decided to protest military recruitment among impressionable young people.

Aaron was fervently anti-military, as he saw all the expenditures on war as a waste when there were children going to bed hungry at night. He deduced that the whole idea of fighting communism was nothing but a giant farce perpetrated by the government and the military-industrial complex to keep the people in fear, so that they could be more easily manipulated. So, much like the Islamophobia practiced in the USA recently, the communist threat was blown out of proportion. In fact, the only threat the communists posed was the threat of showing the inherent cruelty of the capitalistic system that promoted greed as an enviable trait.

This intense dislike of militarism had actually brought Aaron and Casey together in forming a small group of students to protest the military being permitted to brainwash students, stir up their patriot fervour, and then get them to sign, with their equally easily manipulated parents, an agreement to enter the military after graduation from high school. It is important that this be mentioned here, because this is the singular event that would serve as a catalyst to motivate Aaron and Casey to undertake an investigation that would rock the very foundations of Asheboro society. Without these two people forming an alliance to protest the military on campus, the ghost of Sue Ann McGee may not have been stirred up again.

Aaron, more excited about spending time with Casey than he was protesting the military on campus, often looked longingly at her as if he was in a trance. Casey was speaking about the plans to Aaron and their six compatriots when she noticed that he was not listening to her, but rather seemed more interested in staring at her chest. She snapped her fingers in front of his face and said, "Earth to Aaron – come in Aaron. This is serious business; I need your attention."

Aaron, sitting up straight and shaking his head, replied, "Yeah, yeah, I'm sorry, I was thinking about how we are going to keep this secret for two days. If the principal gets wind of this, he will shut it down faster than the sheriff closes up the striptease show when the carnival comes to town. Remember when we all were wearing our shirttails out? Mr. Turkian looked at the act of pulling your shirttail out as nothing less than subversion. In a society that makes its youth stand and blindly recite the pledge of allegiance every day, that act of rebellion could not be tolerated, and he shut it down right away. What we are planning now is even worse. I'm telling you that we are all going to get expelled."

Casey was surprised by Aaron's outburst. "What are you saying Aaron? You want to back out now? Of course we will be expelled. It will only be for 3 days, a week at the most. Isn't it worth it to make a statement against militarism? We are talking about an organization that is taking young people, indoctrinating them, actually brainwashing them into dying for a bunch of corporations that make money off war."

Aaron, ashamed that he had faltered for an instance, was resolute with his reply. "No, I am not backing out. I am in it to the end. I was just making sure we all know what will happen to us. We are told what a free country this is, but every time someone tries to exercise freedom, the church, the government or some corporate entity tries to shut you up. The principal represents the establishment, and the establishment wants everyone to do exactly as told. We only have freedom as long as we don't demand it. When we demand it, there will be dire consequences, because people who think for themselves are a threat."

Casey, now reassured of Aaron's commitment to the cause, smiled and gave him a little wink with her left eye. "That's my old Aaron – filled with the revolutionary spirit and ranting about the lack of freedom in this country. Let's go over our plans one more time."

Casey, very carefully laid out what would occur. "First, the army, navy, marines and air force will all be side-by-side in the gym – sections A, B, C and D. Across the court from them will be in Section E, Eric Parson from Parson manufacturing. Section F will be the Newspaper spokesperson. Section G will be Guilford Dairy, and section H will be Dr. Bryson. Joe and Bill, you will be in line at section E and F. Ann and Bob, you will be in the back of the line at section G, and Roberta and Ray, you will be in line at section H. Aaron and I will be just inside the hallway near the locker room at the entrance to the gym. Aaron and I will walk out, shouting 'down with militarism – up with social programmes.' Then, all six of you will turn around, join us at mid court and we will all shout the slogan together until someone removes us. My guess is that they will not call the police, but remember that they will have a spokesperson here, so there will be a police person in the building. Anyway, we will shout the slogan as long as we can. Do not stop, even when they are physically removing you."

White Meteors and the Ghost of Sue Ann McGee

The most important part of the plan was the placement of Aaron and Casey in the corridor near the locker room. That would make it possible for two inquisitive people to finally explore the truth about what had been termed an accident for so many years. Soon, Aaron and Casey would be tracking down a murderer.

Aaron had a glow about him when he walked out of school with Casey by his side. He felt euphoric just being in her presence. Although he was immensely concerned about the direction of a country that seemed hell-bent on subjugating the entire population to religious, economic and patriotic servitude, Aaron was, in this particular case, ruled more by hormones than his commitment to social justice. Despite his distaste for the way the military preyed on impressionable youths to fill its ranks, his primary motivation for interest in the Career Day protest was the opportunity to be near Casey.

On the other hand, Casey's motives were more altruistic. She was from a wealthy family that owned more real estate than anyone in town. Her father's investments in the stock market had made him one of the wealthiest men in Asheboro. Her two brothers were successful businessmen in Charlotte and Greensboro, and her father was grooming her to be something a bit unusual for women of the era, an attorney. Although she had every intention of becoming a lawyer, her goal was to work for the poor, not be the corporate attorney that her father had in mind. The two of them often had heated arguments about the lack of social justice in America, and how the wealthy always reaped the benefits of capitalism on the backs of the middle class and poor who picked up the tab.

Although a member of the upper class, she definitely did not represent the typical upper class mentality. She was a young woman with a conscience and a deep abiding belief that any system that let the majority of benefits flow to those at the top simply denied the vast majority the economic and social fairness to which all human beings should be entitled. She was truly a young woman who hungered for justice.

Career Day saw Eric Parson return to the school gym for the first time since the ill-fated graduation ceremony nine years before. He had not even attended any basketball games, because the sight of the gym generated an intense fear in him. However, his father had insisted that he show up for Career Day. Parson manufacturing should have a representative there from the most prominent family in town, and not just an employee, but a Parson. His brothers had done it before, now it was time for him to do it. Franklin Parson was tired of Eric's fear over some ghostly spectre that was nothing but a figment of people's imagination.

What happened that day was not nearly as dramatic as what occurred many times before, but it would serve as a catalyst to motivate Aaron and Casey to uncover an incredible conspiracy of silence that had been going on for nearly ten years. It was a rather sublime occurrence, but the effect would ultimately be incredibly dramatic.

As Eric Parson set-up his table to discuss job opportunities with Parson manufacturing, he kept casting a weary eye toward the entryway to the corridor, where so much mayhem had occurred years before. He caught himself staring at the locker room door and felt a definite uneasiness as his heart raced and his breathing became shallower. Then, he turned his back for a few seconds to walk behind the desk and take a seat. While he was doing so, Aaron and Casey looked about the now filling gym and surreptitiously slipped into the corridor and stepped behind the right wall, completely out of site. They waited patiently for the military people to set-up their booths in preparation for their propagandizing efforts to lure the poor and blindly patriotic into serving in the military as the country was preparing to engage in an illegal and immoral war in a small backwards country called Vietnam.

Eric Parson sat behind his fold-out desk and tried to avert his eyes from the corridor of horror that had haunted him for so long. He lowered his head and just stared at the desk, seemingly in deep, contemplative thought. While he was doing so, Aaron and Casey stood side-by-side in the corridor. Aaron intentionally pivoted on his left foot a bit so his body would slightly touch Casey. Casey, alert to what he was attempting, grimaced a bit, but decided she would let him get away with it. After all, he was a really nice young man, and was intensely enamoured with her. And she did have feelings for him, although they were not as intense as his. She found herself wondering what it would be like to kiss him.

About 10 metres down the hallway to Aaron's right and behind him was a full-length mirror. For some reason, Aaron felt an irresistible urge to look to his right and down the hallway. There was no one in the corridor and the lights, as usual, were turned off and only a faint flicker of sunlight filtered through the small, thick, double class in the fortress-like steel door at the end of the dark and gloomy hall. Aaron squinted his eyes and looked in the mirror. His heart began to palpitate furiously as he saw an image of a woman. He could not see any face, for her back was turned to the mirror. Yet, when he looked away from the mirror, there was no one standing in front of it. Looking back at the mirror, he noticed the girl was tall, and he thought the blackness of her hair seemed to be lost in the equally dark blackness of the shadows in the mirror. The figure was dressed in white and there was a breeze that seemed to blow gently making her dress flutter, along with her hair. Aaron blinked his eyes and shook his head hoping to clear up the fog of his mind that was playing tricks on him and the figure vanished like the flame of a candle vanishes, or as the breath vanishes from the mirror that has been breathed upon. Confused, Aaron could not bring himself to share his vision with Casey. He shook his head a couple of times, as if clearing the vision from his brain. Casey looked at him in a bewildered fashion and whispered, "what's wrong, Aaron?"

Aaron, not wanting to admit to seeing things that weren't there, replied, "Nothing, nothing, isn't it about time?"

"No, wait until the gym is completely filled, then we step out and start our chant," replied Casey.

Casey felt a sudden rush of cold air behind her, and looked to her right and saw a ghostly figure open the locker room door and disappear inside. She was in such shock that she could only softly utter, "her, it's her."

Aaron looked down at Casey and said, "What do you mean, it's her?"

Casey slightly shivering replied, "you wouldn't believe me if I told you."

Aaron, sensing that she had seen what he had previously observed, said, "You saw the figure of a woman in white. Am I right?"

Casey could not muster the words as they seemed to stick in her throat. All she did was nod her head affirmatively. Aaron, never one to be fearful of anything whispered, "What did you see?"

"I saw her go into the locker room," replied Casey.

"Do you know her?"

"Aaron, I have seen pictures of her in my brother's high school yearbook."

Aaron, realizing her brothers were seven and nine years older than she was, said, "so, what is a girl from the 50's doing wandering the hallway?"

Slightly grimacing and shaking her head, Casey replied, "You don't understand. I got a look at her face – the side of her face. There is a profile picture of her in my brother Earl's yearbook. She is shown with the pep band at a basketball game. The picture shows her profile. I know the profile, because I have heard the story of her from my brother for years. Aaron, it was Sue Ann McGee."

Aaron, fighting back laughter, because he did not want to do anything that would hurt Casey, whispered, "well, maybe you saw someone who reminded you of the yearbook picture, but believe me Casey, it was not Sue Ann McGee. I know all the stories, but dead people just aren't in the habit of getting out of the grave and walking around our high school."

Casey, herself, not one who believed any of the outlandish tales she had heard over the years, got very pensive and said, "I don't believe in ghosts either Aaron, but I know what I saw. You game to go into the locker room?"

Aaron, concerned about their primary objective, somewhat sarcastically replied, "Aren't you forgetting the real reason we are here?"

"Aaron, you and I both know that no one really cares about the coming war. Thousands of young American boys will be killed, and millions of Vietnamese slaughtered because the government always keeps people fearful that someone is going to take away our freedom. No one wants to take our freedom except the people in our own country who manipulate us every day. We are just voices crying in the wilderness. There are too few of us willing to take a stand. Forget the demonstration; let's see if we can solve a mystery that has been plaguing this school for years. What about it? You are always playing private investigator. How many times do I heard you talk about *77 Sunset Strip*, *Surfside Six* and *Bourbon Street Beat*. Those are just television detective shows. Come on, be a real detective. Let's go into that locker room."

Aaron, titillated by the thought of spending time with Casey, enthusiastically replied, "Let's do it Casey. Let's get to the bottom of this ghost malarkey."

Casey smiled, took Aaron by the hand, much to his delight, and led him toward the locker room and what would become the greatest adventure of their lives.

The locker room door opened with a creaking noise. The room was totally dark. Aaron fiddled around for the light switch and flicked it on. The lights came on in the front part of the large room, but the back, where the showers were, was still dark. The two of them surveyed the room right, left, up and down. They walked around the lockers, stopped and looked at one another quizzically. Then, the lights in the shower room came on and a lone shower could be heard. The water was so hot that steam began to rise toward the ceiling. Aaron and Casey crept slowly forward toward the shower stalls.

A slight breeze blew from the shower area and steam floated over the tiled wall separating the showers from the rest of the locker room. Aaron reached down and took Casey's hand. She willingly placed her hand in his, not out of fear, but out of a feeling of comradeship.

As the slight breeze blew the steam laden sullen air their way, an outline of a woman seemed to be forming above the tiled wall and a slight sigh could be faintly heard. It was almost as if someone was pleading. Yes, they were pleading, whispering quietly, almost crying for someone who cared, genuinely cared about the misery that was overwhelming them.

Slight moisture formed in Aaron and Casey's eyes. They were so saddened by the intense sighing and moaning that their hearts ached with pain for the soul that was crying out in misery. Yet, they both felt great trepidation as they slowly crept toward the shower stalls, waiting to come face-to-face with whatever waited for them in all that steam.

The air suddenly smelled of rot and decay. For years, the stories of a thing that walked the dark, deep lonely corridor of despair had been told and retold until the tales had faded into to the twilight of legend. Now, Aaron and Casey were about to face the flittering phantom as they drew near the opening to the showers. A chilling shiver ran down Casey's spine as she reached out with her left hand and strongly gripped Aaron's right hand. This time, Aaron did not muster his usual hormonal urges, as the grip he held on Casey's hand was one of a protective nature, wanting to shield her from any harm that might be lurking in the steam behind the wall.

The two of them did not speak, as all their concentration was focused on what they were about to face. Casey placed her right hand over her nose in an attempt to blot out the overwhelming stench that was permeating the slight breeze that was blowing from the shower area.

Aaron instinctively remembered something that his Uncle Wayne, a writer, had once penned in one of his novels, "the wind blows hot and cold, laden with both evil and good. Guard against the wind of doom. You may not, shall not, can not ever whisper into the wind. Tread lightly, silently to face that which abides in the wind."

CHAPTER 4
PURSUIT OF JUSTICE FOR SUE ANN McGEE

Close your eyes, darkness is deep.
My killers are in peaceful sleep.
Inside their hearts, no remorse,
But they did not reckon a ghostly force.

Mirrors of lies chant my name.
They will now play my ghostly game.
Nightmares will flow through their minds,
Because ghostly spectres build my shrines.

Their evil deed imprisons me.
I need the truth for all to see.
Murder was my earthly fate.
Only justice will free me, so I wait.

Aaron and Casey were committed to finding out what horror was behind the tile wall that separated the lockers from the showers. As they got to the tile wall, they started to turn to the right and the shower instantly ceased. All that could be heard was the gurgling sound of water as it cascaded down the drain. No whining, no sighing, no crying, no moaning, just the silence penetrated by the gurgling water. Then it, too, ceased. The steam was dissipating, and they moved through it toward the shower that had been on, the water still slightly pooling around the shower head and then dropping to the tile floor. Behind the showers was a row of sinks, and above them mirrors that were now filled with the moisture from the steam. Focusing on the sink in the middle of the row, they both noticed what appeared to be writing on the mirror above it.

They stood before the sink and their hearts raced with excitement. In all capital letters, printed on the mirror in the moisture from the steam was one word – *MURDER*.

.

The word slowly faded into oblivion as the moisture dissipated and little beads of water ran down the mirror. They heard a rustling noise in the locker room, turned and hurriedly left the shower area to see what it was. As they got to the locker room, the door to it was closing. All they caught was a brief glimpse of a ghostly figure, as the door closed behind it.

Running to the door, they looked out into the corridor, down toward the exit door at the end and there was nothing. Looking back the other way, all they saw was their compatriots, who had expected them to lead the demonstration, being physically removed by the soldiers, who had apparently decided to use some of their military training against a new enemy – students who were practicing the freedom the soldiers were supposed to be defending. Their friends were staring back at them in disgust, and it would take many weeks for them to forgive Casey and Aaron for not taking part in the demonstration, but for now, the two were too mystified about what had occurred to do anything but agree to meet at Hop's Bar-B-Q at 6:00 PM to go over the events of the day.

Casey and Aaron headed off to class, as the demonstration had ended the Career Day early and would long be remembered as the first demonstration against the American war machine at the high school. There would be more, and they would all be met by the same intolerance for freedom that greeted Americans protesting the war for years. All across America, many students would be beaten, brutalized, jailed and even killed by government authorities and their representatives, intent on squelching any attempt by young people to exercise the very rights that they were told the communists were trying to destroy. This hypocrisy was planting the seeds of discontent that would foster many to take bold stands against the military-industrial complex that was the chief beneficiary of wars.

That night, Aaron spent a great deal of time primping for what he considered his first date with Casey Felton. As always when a big date came up, a nasty pimple would appear. He borrowed some of his mother's makeup and dabbed it on his cheek, mostly concealing it. Those hormones just never stopped causing trouble.

Aaron thought that maybe Hop's wasn't the classiest dining establishment in town, but it was a start. After all, it was Casey who suggested it, and it certainly wouldn't put too big a crimp in Aaron's wallet. He entertained the idea that after a sandwich at Hop's, maybe he could convince her to go to the Sunset Theatre next door for a movie. Thinking back over the day, he was more excited about holding Casey's hand than the writing that appeared on the mirror or the spectre they thought they might have seen. Yeah, he had actually held her dainty little hand in his. Oh boy, those hormones were starting to kick in again.

Casey knew that her father would not take kindly to her going out with Aaron, even if it wasn't what she thought of as a date. Her father knew the reputation of Aaron's father as a lady's man, so he figured like father like son, so Casey would have had to endure one of his tirades about sullying the family name by being seen with someone like Aaron. Normally, she would have stood up to him, but this time, she thought it best to avoid a confrontation. Consequently, she told Aaron to meet her at Hop's to avoid her father.

Hop's was a favourite of all the people in Asheboro who enjoyed what was referred to as "down home cooking." Toiling away preparing old-fashioned "greasy spoon" food was Burt Hop, a gregarious, rotund man who always had his white apron on and a perpetual smile, as he waved hello to the patrons from behind the grill. His wife, Lauralee, was by the front door, sitting at the cash register to greet the diners. This night, she was surprised to see Aaron walk in so late. He usually dropped by only on Saturdays when he worked at Jones' Department Store, which was downtown. Many times, Lauralee would let Aaron's bill slide for a week or so when he was low on money. She smiled and said, "Well Aaron, I am not used to seeing you so late in the day or so early in the week. What brings you out tonight?"

Aaron, somewhat proud of the fact he was going to meet Casey, said rather boastfully, "have a date with Casey Felton tonight. Tell Burt to give us an extra big helping of Bar-B-Q when we order."

Lauralee could not help but grin as she said, "Well, I guess you finally pulled it off. I have heard that you were pretty sweet on Casey. You must have worked that old Adam's charm on her."

Aaron shrugged his shoulders, sort of bowed his head sheepishly and replied, "Could you show her where I am when she comes in?"

Lauralee, winking at Aaron, pointed to a booth all the way in the back corner and said, "Go back there, Aaron. It will be more private."

Aaron meandered toward the booth, euphoric with anticipation that after all those years he was actually going to sit across from Casey Felton on a date. Well, maybe not a real date, it was more of a meeting, but in his mind it was an almost date – yeah, an almost date.

Sitting in the booth anxiously awaiting Casey's arrival, he kept staring toward the entrance with anticipatory delight. Pretty soon, the most beautiful girl in Asheboro would walk through the door and sit across from him. He would have to exude self-confidence and savoir faire. Yeah, that's what it was, savoir faire. It denoted a certain style, accomplishment and refinement that only sophisticated people had. He had read about it in a book about France once. He was going to be the coolest guy Casey had ever been out with. This was Aaron's chance. He couldn't blow it!

Then, there she was, standing by the cash register as Lauralee pointed toward Aaron's booth. Taller than most 17 year old girls at almost 6 feet, Casey's smooth, confident strides that accentuated her long, muscular legs made Aaron go into a Byron-like trance as he recited to himself: *She walked in beauty, like the night. She was of cloudless climes and starry skies. She was all that is best of dark and bright as I gazed upon her heavenly eyes. She was mellowed to the tender light that softly lightens her face where thoughts serenely, sweetly express how pure and dear was their dwelling place. On her soft cheeks and her brow so fine, calmness and eloquence tell of days in goodness spent and a heart sweet and innocent. Yes, she walked in beauty, like the night and she was of cloudless climes and starry skies.*

Aaron sat in blissful ecstasy as she slid gracefully into the booth, her figure of perfect elegance making his heart pound furiously. Her most impressive feature was her dark and abundant hair, so glossy that it threw off the sunshine with a gleam flickering through the window by the booth. Her complexion was rich, her eyes dark and deep and what a beautiful countenance. In fact, so physically stunning was she to Aaron's eyes that her beauty shone out, and made a halo of the misfortune and ignominy in which the two were about to be enveloped.

To Aaron, since the second grade, she was the caress of desire, the soothing sweetness of affection shed over life's toils, a reflection of the true beauty of soul that was possible but nearly extinct in the human race. In her, there was a treasure of consoling tenderness to allay every pain. She was an initiator of hope in Aaron. She exuded utopian confidence and faith in the possibilities of life and above all, in love and inspirational desire to create a paradise of perfection and the power of reaching toward it step by step with assured confidence. She was pleasing to the eye, which, no doubt, made her a sparkling jewel, but more importantly, she was pleasing to the heart, which made her a treasure to be savoured.

Sitting there in front of Aaron, beauty's brightest colours had decked her out in all the hues of heaven. Of course, she was accustomed to the attention of men and even many women, but everyone has a different idea of beauty, and this day Aaron saw the shadow of a magnificent branch and his mind was flowing freely to create the tree that went with it. There is in every true woman's heart, a spark of heavenly fire, which lies dormant in the broad daylight of reality, but on this day, sitting in front of Aaron, Casey kindled, beamed and blazed like a beacon in the dark of night. She was an air of the divine to Aaron through which all her gentle graces shined. The magnificent body charmed and titillated, but it was the soul that spoke of perfection. Yes, he admired her shapely limbs and perfectly proportioned body, but they were the flowers that would have their dated hours as years went by. Aaron knew that they were but momentary sweets that would wilt with the passing of time. It was the stainless soul within that outshone the fairest of outward beauty.

Somewhat embarrassed by the mesmerized gaze of Aaron, Casey interjected her favourite refrain when young men were overwhelmed by her beauty. "Earth to Aaron, come in Aaron."

Aaron, snapping out of his trance, noticed people at the nearby booths were staring at him. He said, "how rude, Casey. How rude I am. Please forgive me."

Casey, smiling intently replied, "Aaron, it is O.K., but one day you are going to realize that I simply am not interested in you romantically."

Aaron, feeling foolish that he thought he was actually on a date with Casey, had no response. He bit the right side of his lower lip as Casey reached across the table, took his hand and stared into his eyes. "Aaron, you are a dear boy, maybe the dearest boy in the whole school, because I know that, like me, you have a big soft spot in your heart for the poor and downtrodden who get no justice in a country designed to serve those at the top. I also know I attract the attention of many boys, and I make no secret that I enjoy it. What normal person wouldn't? However, I also know that physical beauty can be vain and doubtfully of any lasting good. It is nothing but a shiny gloss that fades with time. Get over your infatuation and let's get down to doing something important to eradicate what may have been a gross injustice."

Aaron, gaining his composure, basked in the attention she was showing him, even if it wasn't romantic. He smiled and said, "Your body charms the eyes Casey, but believe me, it is the soul I really see. I am not just a captive of your face and body. I see your real grace, and it is a pleasure to call you friend, even if that is all you will ever be to me."

Casey, let go of his hand, leaned back in the seat and whispered softly, "You are something special Aaron Adams and I like the way you think, but you are a man, so, with all due respect, I still think you are more attracted to my body than my soul. However, let's leave it at that and have some good old Hop's Barbecue."

Aaron nodded in the affirmative, and signalled for Lauralee, who strolled over to take their order. She looked down at Aaron and gave him a little wink. She was a romantic at heart and had a real affinity for all the young people who came to Hop's to do their courting.

After eating their delicious barbecue, Casey asked Aaron where they should start their investigation, and Aaron's answer surprised her. "First should be Miss Fields. Why did she pick Sue Ann McGee that day to be first up the rope? If another person had gone up it, then we wouldn't be talking about Sue Ann McGee's death. It would be someone else's."

"O.K., but how do we approach her?"

Aaron leaned over the table and whispered softly, "we go by her office right after school. We tell her that we are doing a paper for English class and we want to talk about some things that have happened at the school in the past, and since she has been here over 30 years, it is only logical that she could provide us with some interesting stories about what went on in the 40's and 50's. When we get to the 50's, then we bring up Sue Ann McGee's death."

Casey, nodded her head in agreement, and then really surprised Aaron with a suggestion he was totally unprepared for. "Sounds good. Hey, it is almost 7 o'clock. You pay for the meal, and I will pay for the movie. That is if you promise to keep your hands to yourself in the dark."

Aaron, thrilled she would consider going to the movies with him replied, "Casey, I will be a perfect gentleman. I assure you that my obnoxious behaviour earlier will never occur again."

Casey, mischievously tilting her head to one side, replied, "Well Aaron, you don't have to be a perfect gentleman. That would make me think I was losing my appeal. Just know that I won't permit things to go too far, because I know what boys always have on their minds. We are friends, not lovers."

Aaron couldn't believe that she was actually engaging in romantic banter with him. She had no interest she said, but still she was willing to spend the evening with him at the movies. Maybe, just maybe Aaron could spark that interest if he were cagey enough. Ah, he thought, hope springs eternal. And just hearing her say the word "lovers" gave him a queasy feeling in the pit of his stomach.

Even at the age of 17, Aaron was not one to quiver in awe before authority. His father had often told him to never be afraid to ask anyone "why" when told to do something, even if it was a teacher. "Those," said his father, "who refuse to ask why are destined to always let others do their thinking for them. If a person can not tell you why you should do something, then it is not worth doing. And do not accept a reason without investigating it yourself. Always question a person's motives. If more Americans asked why their government insisted on witch hunts against communists, perhaps there would not be so much fear of that which people did not understand. Instead of accepting government propaganda about communism, read the Communist Manifesto, and decide for yourself. *Why* is the most important word in the English language."

With that in mind, Aaron and Casey went to see Miss Fields, with one critical question containing the word *why* on their minds.

Agreeing to discuss the past with them, Miss Fields had no idea where it would ultimately lead, but just as she had finished talking about the magnificent championship football season in 1953, Casey got to the crux of the conversation. She tried to be as diplomatic as possible as she said, "Miss Fields, we know it must be traumatic for you, but we would like to discuss Sue Ann McGee's death, and why you think the grappling rope broke that day at the particular time she was using it."

Miss Fields stood up with an irate look on her face and pointed toward the door. "Out! Out of my office, now. This conversation is finished."

Aaron, his furtive mind racing with questions that were forming as a result of Miss Fields sudden outburst, said, "Sure, we will get out, but don't think this will end our investigation. We are going to find out the truth about Sue Ann McGee, with or without your assistance."

Miss Fields, now seething with anger, screamed, "Aaron Adams, you don't want to mess with me. I'll have you in the principal's office faster than you can blink an eye. Sue Ann McGee was killed in a horrible accident. There is no need to drag up a horrible incident like that. Too many people could be hurt."

Aaron, making sure to stay polite and respectful, said, "I apologize if we upset you, Miss Fields, but there is something strange about her death, and even sending me to the principal will not diminish our enthusiasm to explore and probe into that death. You are the girl's PE teacher, so you have never had me in class. Ask your colleague, Mr. Hurt, the men's PE teacher, about me. I am not a great athlete, but I have determination. In basketball, in soccer, in lacrosse, in track, whatever the sport, he will tell you I always give my all, regardless of my lack of ability. I am not a quitter, and I will not quit on this quest, any more than I would quit in the 1500 metre run at the track meet last year. I was so exhausted I had to crawl to the finish line, but I did it. I am tenacious if not talented. I am going to find out the truth about Sue Ann McGee, with or without your input."

Miss Fields, somewhat calmer, motioned for Aaron and Casey to sit back down. "O.K. Aaron, I am going to tell you all I know about the accident. I have told the police, but I am going to share it with you and Casey. It has been nearly 10 years now, but that day haunts me constantly, but it was an accident, just a horrible accident. Of that I am sure."

Casey leaned forward with intense interest and said, "We do not mean to make you suffer any anguish. I can tell you that we are not out to harm anyone."

Miss Fields, always presented a gruff exterior, but she seemed more approachable now. It was as if a complete change in personality had taken place. Her arrogance was gone and she seemed more sedate.

"You both know the Parson family, obviously. Well, there were intensely bad feelings between Eric Parson and Sue Ann McGee. It had been going on for many months. It was something about a run-in they had one day when Eric apparently parked in the bus-parking zone and Sue Ann said something to him about it. In my opinion, Sue Ann should probably have kept her mouth shut and gone on into class. Eric was a bit arrogant sometimes, but I always found him and his family to be exceedingly nice. Anyway, this disagreement apparently spiralled out of control to the point that Eric's girlfriend, Mary Lou Hinton nearly came to blows with Sue Ann one day and they both wound up in the principal's office. I had both Mary Lou and Sue Ann in my advanced PE class for seniors who needed one extra credit for graduation. It was a pretty easy class, just a few exercise routines once a week for an hour. The morning of the accident, it was well-known that the students would be going up the grappling rope one by one and getting a grade based upon how high up they got. Despite what the rumour is, I did not pick Sue Ann to go up first that morning. The list was prepared the week before, and each student knew when their turn would be. Sue Ann was first, because she was always one of the worst students athletically. I picked the weakest students first when I made out the list, because I wanted to make sure the weakest ones would get another chance later if they were not able to succeed. I must admit that I rarely checked the rope, and I certainly didn't on that day, other than wiggling it a little bit. Sue Ann knew she was first. So, she grabbed the rope and surprised us all as she made her way all the way to the top. In fact, she was receiving applause from most of the students for her accomplishment. Then, things went terribly wrong."

Aaron interjected, "Did she give any indication that she knew she was going to fall?"

"Aaron, she was at the very top, a good thirty feet off the floor. She looked up at the beam, and apparently saw the flayed rope and knew she was going to fall. She looked down at me, and I could see the fear in her eyes. She just fell to the floor, and she never moved afterward. I tried CPR, but there was no response, no response whatsoever. She died instantly." Then Miss Fields bowed her head a bit as if in contemplative thought and continued. "Regardless of who would have been up there, I would have felt responsible, because I made out the list. She did not even scream. It was as if she knew she was going to die and just accepted her fate."

Even at the age of 17, Aaron's investigative instincts were sharp. He looked directly into Miss Field's eyes and said, "So, the list was out for one week prior to the accident?"

"Yes, I posted it on the bulletin board by the door."

Aaron felt he was now onto something really important and had a tinge of excitement in his next question. "So, for one week, the entire student body could have read the list. Even people who just happened by the school and walked into the gym had access to the list."

Suddenly, Miss Fields was aware of just where Aaron was heading with his questioning. "Yes Aaron, it was up there for all to see, but the Chief-of-Police investigated, and determined it was an accident – an accident."

Aaron's next statement had to be carefully phrased, because he did not want to raise the ire of Miss Field's again. "You say it was an accident, the chief says it was an accident, the principal at the time said it was an accident, even Sue Ann's parents apparently believed it was an accident. The only problem is that she was pregnant, and there is no one who came forward to claim he was the father of the baby that was also killed in the fall. It just seems that there are a lot of unanswered questions that should be explored." He then got up, motioned for Casey to join him, and made one final statement. "Miss Fields, Casey and I are not afraid of adversity. We are not fearful of authority, and we have been informed by an anonymous source that Sue Ann McGee's fall was no accident. We are committed to finding out the truth."

Miss Fields, her arrogant manner returning, stood and said, "You will both be sorry if you keep sticking your noses into affairs that are best left alone. You, Aaron, are known for challenging authority, but Casey, you have a stellar reputation. Aaron will only get you in trouble. You are jeopardizing your good standing with the faculty and your peers by hanging around with him."

It was then that Casey endeared herself forever to Aaron, when she said, "Miss Fields, I am proud to stand by Aaron's side. He is my friend, and he is a boy who refuses to let convention stand in the way of doing the right thing. Aaron Adams is the very embodiment of what all young men should be. He will not bow before the tyranny of the privileged class in school, at work, at church or anywhere else where justice is denied."

The two of them left the room, slamming the door behind them. Aaron glanced at Casey and smiled as they walked down the hallway. She grinned and said, "Don't get too cocky, Aaron Adams."

Aaron did not reply. He just smiled and thought that he and Casey were going to be a formable team in the pursuit of justice for Sue Ann McGee.

CHAPTER 5
TRUTH"S SANCTITY

The grimness of the grave
held the truth in abeyance.
Still, truth rose from its trap.
It looked upon the sullen world
to see only lies and deceit.
But alas, there is a seeker of truth.
He is a breath, a wind,
a shadow, a phantom.
Long shall he pursue truth,
undeterred by the mountain of lies.
He shall know truth's sanctity.

One of the most maligned students in the school was an effeminate and openly gay young man named Gillie Gilberts. For today's modern urban youths, it might be difficult to comprehend just how difficult it was to be gay in a small southern town in the 1960's. To say Gillie's life was often a living hell would be an understatement. This was still an era when students had to listen to a morning devotional from the Bible over the public address system, as separation of church and state was simply something written on a paper called the U.S. Constitution, but was never really practiced, especially in the Bible Belt of America, where elementary schools required classes on the Bible. Consequently, almost all students pointed the finger of condemnation at Gillie, because he just happened to be gay, and the Bible, at least according to those who interpreted it for those unwilling to read it and interpret it for themselves, said that God saw homosexuality as an abomination.

One might question what this has to do with Aaron and Casey's investigation into the death of Sue Ann McGee. That which seems inconsequential can often have a profound effect on events. Aaron was one of the few in school who befriended Gillie. Although Aaron knew that being friends with Gillie would cause others to point the finger of condemnation at him and by association, accuse him of being a homosexual, he was, even in adolescence, unconcerned with what others thought. He was never one who judged people. Well, as long as they themselves were not judgmental. He deplored those who thought their way was the only way. That was one reason he defiantly befriended Gillie. He simply was disgusted that people would ostracize someone because of their sexual orientation. In an era before it was acceptable to realize that sexual orientation was not a choice, Aaron was far ahead of others in accepting people regardless of their sexual orientation. In fact, he was a true friend of all the outsiders who were often ridiculed by fellow students. Aaron was indeed a friend of the friendless, and so was Casey.

On the day after the confrontation with Miss Fields, Gillie, who sat beside Aaron in Miss Powell's English class, was being taunted by a student named Wild Bill McCloud. Aaron, not a particularly imposing figure, and not overly athletic, never backed down from a fight. In fact, he had once fought Wild Bill in the infamous "coal bin" where students were allowed to go between classes and smoke. Yes, that is correct, in the south of the early 1960's, students were actually allowed to smoke on campus as North Carolina was the home of the cigarette corporations that were catered to like royalty by a government that saw addiction to a drug as just good business. Anyway, Wild Bill and he had fought over a relatively minor thing, something to do with Aaron showing him disrespect by flipping him off when Wild Bill cut in front of him in line. Wild Bill had literally beat Aaron to a pulp, knocking him down numerous times, but each time Aaron would get up and take more punishment. Finally, with Aaron refusing to stay down, even once crawling to Wild Bill's leg and swinging at it with his fists, Wild Bill finally shook his head, turned around and walked away in frustration that Aaron would not quit.

From that day forward, although not his friend, Wild Bill actually developed a great deal of respect for Aaron. So, when Wild Bill said to Gillie, "You need to start wearing a dress to school. That way you might attract more boyfriends," Aaron gave him a stern look and said, "Well, Bill, at least he can attract something besides dogs. Do the dogs you date wear dresses?"

Wild Bill puffed out his chest and replied, "Aaron, you want to spend the rest of this class picking up your teeth?"

Aaron, as always, simply refused to back down. "Let's go the coal bin and you can wear your hands out on my face."

Wild Bill laughed, and said, "No thanks, the last time exhausted me." Then, he turned to Gillie and said, "Sorry Gillie, you are what you are, and if it is OK with Aaron, it is OK with me. Aaron has character. He has no fighting ability, but he has character. You're lucky to have him as a friend."

Aaron offered another witticism: "Wild Bill, if you keep at it, you might wind up being a pretty decent fellow."

Wild Bill replied, "Don't count on it!"

So, that day, Gillie found another friend in Wild Bill, who decided that like Aaron, he was through with worrying about what others thought. Gillie was an alright guy, and there was no reason why he should make fun of him. The significance of this will become clearer as the story unfolds. Patience is a virtue.

That evening, around 6:00 PM, Aaron and Casey went to visit Mary and Frank McGee, who were still living in the converted barn. Surprised by their visit, when Aaron said that they wanted to talk to them about Sue Ann's death, they seemed reluctant. It was then that Casey said, "I do not want to alarm you, but a strange thing happened to us a couple of days ago. If you will listen to what happened, I think you may understand why it is imperative that we talk to you."

For the next few minutes, she and Aaron described to them the strange occurrences in the locker room. Enthralled and captivated, the two parents broke down in tears as they tried to fathom what was happening. They assumed that the death of their daughter was simply an event that was long forgotten, but now these two young people had decided to delve into what might not have been an accident after all.

Aaron, showing deep concern for Mrs. McGee, who was wiping tears from the corner of her left eye, said,

"We don't want to cause you any hurt, but we are determined to find out what really happened. There are some questions we need to ask that might be painful, even seemingly disrespectful, but believe me; we have nothing but the best intentions in mind to give your daughter the justice that we think she may have been denied. I know you look upon us just as kids, but we are both 17, soon to be 18 and we are mature for our ages, although our parents might argue the point. Don't take our youth as an indication that we aren't capable of conducting a credible investigation. Anyway, unfortunately, we are probably the only ones interested, besides yourselves, in finding out the truth about what really happened."

Mr. McGee looked at Aaron with tears still in his eyes. "Aaron, you and Casey are the only two people who have even mentioned our daughter in years. She died and was forgotten, forgotten by all but us. She was from the wrong side of town to really matter to the authorities. If she had been the daughter of a prominent citizen there would have been a more thorough investigation. But she was just another one of the majority who don't really matter in a world where only the privileged among us get the good educations, the good jobs, the nice homes, all the things that we are told make a person special. My daughter was special, too, but she never got a chance to prove it. She had to struggle for everything she got, because I am a failure in life. Now, I am even a bigger failure, because I have no reason to even try. Our life was destroyed the day my daughter died."

Casey, choking up with emotion as she watched two devastated people seem to wilt into misery before her eyes, said, "We never knew her, but we know that she was a good person whom we think was intentionally killed. For what reason, we are not sure, but we will find out if we possibly can. Just answer Aaron's questions, because he is an astute young man with a penchant for finding things out. He is as tenacious as a bloodhound on the trail of a fox."

Mrs. McGee, choked with emotion, said, "Ask us anything you want Aaron; we desperately need to know the truth, no matter what it is. We have suspected it wasn't an accident, but simply had no proof, and no one willing to help us."

Aaron was more than just an avid investigator. He was an intrepid adolescent Sherlock Holmes with a mind that never ceased in its swirling pursuit of the truth. Once, in history class, when the teacher talked about how magnificent it was that the founders of America coined the phrase "all men are created equal," he asked, "if they thought all men are created equal, then why did all but one of them own slaves? Also, I guess they really meant men, because women were not even given the right to vote until 1920. Maybe they should have also put in there that all men are hypocrites." That outburst cost Aaron two afternoons in detention, but rather than quiet him, it just made him more determined to point out in history class the hypocrisy of a document that simply did not live up to its promises. Along with Casey, Aaron had the highest grades in the class, and his research abilities always made the teacher nervous, because Aaron was one step ahead of him on most things. Aaron learned that a person who was well-prepared could win an argument, not just by superior speaking skills, but by the accumulation of facts to back-up proclamations.

Aaron had prepared all his life to be an investigator. When people asked him, even as a young child, what he wanted to be, his reply was, "I'm going to be a 77 Sunset Stripper." Most people gave him a startled look, because they thought he wanted to be a stripper on Sunset Strip, but what he was really saying, in his own unique way, was that he wanted to be a private detective like Efrem Zimbalist, Jr. and Roger Smith on the television show *77 Sunset Strip*. Granted, part of the appeal was that the detectives were always around beautiful women, but it went beyond that with Aaron. He genuinely enjoyed trying to solve mysteries, no matter how mundane they might be. Now, he was attempting to solve what may well have been a murder.

He very respectfully said to Mr. and Mrs. McGee, "I know it is difficult to talk about this and I wish there were some other way to find the truth, but was their any indication prior to her death that something was bothering Sue Ann?"

"Well, she was a teenager, Aaron," Mrs. McGee said with a slight smile, "so there was the normal turmoil all teenagers face, but for the most part, she was pretty happy. She never really argued with us over anything at all. She was such a good girl, who simply caused us no heartache at all. I can't really think of anything out of the ordinary, no."

"Same here," interjected Mr. McGee.

Aaron, moved gracefully and delicately to the topic that he thought might be a key to the whole thing. "So, even the fact that she was three months pregnant did not seem to alter the way she acted?"

Mrs. McGee replied painfully, "That was strange, because we were open about sexuality. We know that the school is constrained by a society that wants to ignore the fact that sexuality is a part of the human experience and tries to deal with it by keeping kids ignorant. We believed ignorance was a ticket to disaster. That is why we were so shocked when, after her death, we found out she was pregnant. She could have told us and we would have been upset, yes, but she knew that there would have been no recriminations on our part. She understood that she was deeply loved. What is even stranger is that we never saw her with any boy at all during that time. She just wasn't that interested in boys. All she wanted to do was finish high school and then work her way through university. She did not want to wind up like us. She knew this country was not kind to the working men and women, and she wanted to avoid all the despair she saw us suffer, because we weren't smart enough to even get a high school education."

Tears began to flow down Mrs. McGee's cheeks, but she struggled to continue. "We know she was having trouble with Eric Parson and his group of friends. They were making her life hell, but she kept saying that she only had to tolerate it a few more months. Her determination was incredible. We pleaded with her to go to the principal with us, but she said that it would do no good, as the Parson boy and his friends were exempt from the normal rules, because they were part of that class of people who had everything handed to them, had a life made easy by virtue of who their parents were. She knew that people like us simply didn't matter in this world. We just weren't important enough."

When Mrs. McGee said they weren't important enough, it touched a raw nerve in Aaron's social conscience. He indignantly blurted out, "you are important to us, and even though we did not know Sue Ann, she is important to us, too. This country is run by and for those at the top of the economic and social ladder, but the people who really count are people like you, Mr. and Mrs. McGee. Your daughter was not given the justice she deserved, and Casey and I are going to see to it that the truth comes out, no matter who it might affect."

Mr. and Mrs. McGee were impressed by Aaron's maturity and felt that they truly had a champion of justice on their side. Mr. McGee said, "We are here to help you in any way we can. We want to know the truth, no matter what it might be."

Aaron more determined than ever to get the truth, said, "Can you tell me who was at the funeral?"

Mrs. McGee, seeming to be the more articulate of the two, answered, "There were not many from school. There was her best friend, Vicky Martin, Miss Bowdin – the biology teacher, Mr. Hoover – the school janitor, Miss Fields – the PE teacher, Willie Martin – Vicky's uncle and the police chief, Dale Hunter – Sue Ann's lab partner from biology class, and, of course, her uncles, aunts and cousins came from out-of-town. That was all I can think of."

Aaron, looked at an intensely interested Casey, who was frantically writing down all the names Mrs. McGee mentioned in a little pocket notebook and said, "got them all?"

Nodding, Casey replied, "yes."

Aaron then asked the question that would trigger a memory that would be a key to the success of the investigation. "Was their anything either of you saw that was unusual that day at the funeral. Think really hard; was there anything unusual at all – an unusual flower, something unusual said, an unusual individual whom you might not have known. The smallest thing could be critical."

Mr. McGee looked at Mrs. McGee and said, "The figure in a cloak. Tell him about the figure you saw. The one I didn't see."

Mrs. McGee took a deep breath and in a reluctant manner shared the story of the cloaked figure she had seen twice, once in the distance by a tree, and then tossing a flower into the grave as they were preparing to leave the cemetery. Yet, she could not help but include a caveat. "Of course, Frank said I was just imaging things, because I was so overwrought with grief, and he did not see the figure at all. I have put it out of my mind since then, thinking maybe he was right. Maybe it was just my imagination."

Aaron, realizing the significance of what she said, offered a different perspective. "My guess is it wasn't your imagination. In fact, that might well be the father of your daughter's baby. That is the most important thing you have shared with us tonight. We find out who that was, and we are on our way to proving that your daughter's death definitely was no accident. Why was he there, but more important, why was he trying to conceal the fact that he was there?"

Casey's excitement could be clearly seen on her face, and Aaron could not help but smile at her. She was enjoying the investigation as much as he was.

As they prepared to leave, Mrs. McGee could not refrain from asking them a question. "Do you really believe all the stories about Sue Ann haunting that infernal hallway and locker room? We have heard the stories, but just can't bring ourselves to believe in ghosts, but now, you tell us about the strange writing on the shower room mirror and the ghostly figure in the hallway mirror and going in and out the door. We just want to know she is at peace."

Casey, having let Aaron do most of the talking, felt it was her turn to say something. "Mr. and Mrs. McGee, Aaron is more of a sceptic than I am. All I know is what we, ourselves, saw. Was it a ghost? I can't say, but I can tell you that even though I am a religious non-believer, I do believe in the power of good, and unfortunately in the power of evil as well. There was something evil done to your daughter, and you have two people here who will not rest until we exhaust every avenue to get to the truth."

Aaron felt a surge of pride that he could call a person of character like Casey his friend, as Mr. and Mrs. McGee said, "thank you. Thank you, so much."

Aaron was still enamoured with Casey, but now he looked at her as more than just a physically attractive young woman. She was an individual who showed a depth of character that endeared her to him even more, and he begin to feel that she, too, looked upon him in a different way. Maybe, just maybe she was becoming attracted to him.

As Aaron was driving Casey back to her car, which she had parked at Hop's in order to avoid having to confront her father over going out with Aaron, the two enthusiastically reviewed all they had learned from the McGee's. Tomorrow, they would start their investigation into who the strange figure at the graveyard was. Arriving at Hop's, Casey got out, leaned back in the partially opened door and said, "You can pick me up at my house tomorrow morning and take me to school if you want, since we will be going out investigating afterward."

Aaron, shocked that she would allow him to drive up her huge circular driveway to the front of the mansion and pick her up, said, "You sure you want me to do that? I don't think your father is especially fond of me."

"Aaron, my father isn't fond of anyone he thinks isn't from the right social class. You aren't picking him up. You are picking me up. See you tomorrow morning," said Casey as she closed the door and literally skipped to her car, leaving Aaron sitting there, grinning from ear to ear.

The next day Aaron boldly drove up to the front door of the mansion, and Casey walked out with head held high, her lustrous dark hair shimmering in the morning sun. Aaron's thoughts, as he gazed upon her were like raindrops on flowers – beautiful, like a rainbow at a splashing waterfall – beautiful, like a full moon shining through a cloudy sky – beautiful. No matter what beauty his eyes had seen, nothing compared to Casey's beauty.

As she sauntered in front of the car to the other side, she looked through the windshield and smiled at Aaron. She was a wild flower that was rare and beautiful. She stood tall and distinguished among all the women upon whom Aaron had ever gazed. Her natural bubbling beauty was entrancing, and Aaron's heart was palpitating furiously as she sled into the car beside him and said, "Good morning, Sherlock."

Aaron smiled and thought to himself that her honest curiosity and effervescent personality humbled him as he looked beyond her smile and impishness to comprehend the intellectual acuity and warmth that made her a person of substance and style. She was a mirage of wonderment that had captured his heart and soul. He was infected with infatuation, and there was absolutely no cure.

Standing at the living room window, her disapproving father stared daggers at Aaron and her. Casey leaned closer to Aaron, smiled profusely and waved good-bye to her frowning father as she said, "Let's motor Sherlock. We have a mystery to solve, and we aren't going to solve it by sitting here and irritating my father. Put the pedal to the metal."

Pulling into the school parking lot, Aaron noticed a rash of stares from people surprised to see the two of them together. Casey acted as if it was perfectly normal to be with Aaron. Was she just putting on an act of defiance to show her friends how petty they were to be so concerned with social stratification, or was she actually enjoying Aaron's company? Aaron felt that the truth probably lay somewhere in between. She liked him, maybe not romantically, but she did like him. However, she was also the kind of person who loved to make a social statement and flaunt convention. Nonetheless, Aaron was going to enjoy the moment with her regardless of motive. The mystery of Sue Ann McGee was the catalyst that afforded him the opportunity to finally spend time with the one girl he admired above all others.

In English class that morning, Casey and Aaron decided they would need some assistance with their investigation, and they picked two of the most unlikely candidates one could imagine. Sharing lunch with Gillie and Wild Bill, Casey and Aaron noticed the eyes of many wandering their way, confused by the strange fellowship of the school's most socially prominent young lady, the school's resident questioner of authority, the school's toughest part-time thug and the school's flamboyantly gay blade. They all four looked at one another and burst out laughing at themselves. Then, Wild Bill said, "So, what is up. I don't think you invited me and Gillie to share lunch with you just to get stares from other students at the most unlikely foursome anyone could imagine. What gives?"

Aaron, very seriously replied, "Murder is what gives. We're going to solve a murder."

Aaron and Casey told the two enthralled boys about what they had experienced in the hallway and locker room, and then proceeded to share what they had learned from the McGee's the previous night. Aaron, more serious than any of those present were used to seeing him, laid out the plans for an investigation that would rub a lot of people the wrong way. Gillie, excited that he was, in his final few months of school, going to finally be embraced as less than a social pariah by at least three classmates, ecstatically agreed to do whatever he could. In fact, he was so enthusiastic that he was admonished by Casey to not be so exuberant.

Wearing his usual shirt with frills on the sleeves and an unbuttoned top halfway down his hairless chest, Gillie got so excited that he buttoned his shirt up, tucked his frills under his coat sleeve and said, "I'm going to toughen up. This may be dangerous."

All three of the others there could not hold back the laughter, and Aaron offered some advice. "Gillie, you are a fine person, but tough you are not, nor will you ever be. Let Wild Bill take care of any tough stuff. You are to use your brains, not your brawn."

Gillie, realizing his limitations replied, "Gotcha, Aaron."

Wild Bill could not help but ask why they decided on him and Gillie to help, as he offered a frank assessment of their relationship. "Heck, none of us are even friends. You two aren't even really friends unless something is going on I don't know about."

Casey smiled and looked at Aaron before turning back to Wild Bill and saying, "No, we aren't friends or at least we haven't been, but life takes some odd turns on occasion. For some reason, we were thrown together in a situation that seemed to force us to be allies in a search for the truth. Bill, you just happened to be picking on Gillie the other day, and somehow Aaron and I saw that you are a lot more than just the school thug you are made out to be. The way you reached out to Gillie, who has suffered unmerciful teasing and taunting his whole life, simply made us realize that there was a soft heart beneath that gruff exterior. You aren't as tough as you make yourself out to be."

Wild Bill, not used to being considered tender-hearted gruffly said, "Don't let that get around. I wouldn't want to spoil my reputation."

Gillie, always a prankster, effeminately placed his hand on Wild Bill's shoulder and said, "Why big boy, your gruff manner is a real turn-on."

Bill gave him a glare and said, "Don't push it Gillie. I can revert back to my old self in a flash, and you putting your hands on me is not wise."

Gillie couldn't resist. "Hey big boy, you aren't my type, so don't get all huffy on me."

Casey and Aaron, laughed at the bantering between the two, and Casey interjected, "Boys, we have to get down to business. That is if the two of you can cut out the flirting for awhile."

Aaron laid out the plans. He and Casey had already talked to Miss Fields. Next, they were going to find any of Sue Ann's friends still living in the area, starting with Vicky Martin. Gillie and Wild Bill were told to go to the library and get all the information they could from the school yearbook for 1953 about Sue Ann McGee, Eric Parson, Mary Lou Hinton, etc....They were to pour over every picture, every written word that might lead to something connecting anyone to Sue Ann McGee. They were to study the yearbook in detail for anything out of the ordinary in regards to the class of 1953. No matter how innocuous it might seem, they were to make note of it and share the details with Casey and Aaron.

That afternoon, Gillie and Wild Bill made an unusual pair as they walked into the library. Gillie was a dandy supreme as he seemed to float, rather than walk through the doors to the library, dressed in the very tiptop height of fashion. Well, the height of fashion for someone in the court of Louis the Fourteenth that is. Gillie was tall and thin, with a beardless feminine face upon which he always put a bit of rouge, and his light blue eyes seemed to dance with defiance against convention. This was also an era when there was not mass paranoia over fear of weapons being brought into schools, so Gillie often, as he did this day, sported a finely polished coal black cane with a pearl handle. His hands, sticking out from his frilled and laced cuffs were long, thin and dainty to the extreme. Ah, and his nails were long and painted such a bright red that one needed sunglasses to gaze upon them. His tight-fitting pant legs stopped about a foot above the ankle, exposing sock-less, spindly legs that were shaved of all hair. Even the principal had once had his mother in to suggest he dress less flamboyantly, but his mother simply informed the principal that there was no dress code for the school, and that her son would dress as he pleased. And did Gillie dress as he pleased. In fact, that day Wild Bill whispered to him, "Gillie, you've got more guts than any boy in school to dress the way you do."

Gillie, not missing an opportunity for levity, said, "I bet you say that to all the girls."

Wild Bill, the complete opposite in appearance from Gillie; with broad, hulking shoulders on a muscular, tall frame and a rugged slightly pock-marked face with a bit of stubble on it shook his head and said, "Gillie, you just don't know how to take a compliment."

Gillie, realizing that Wild Bill was just trying to be nice and complimentary, replied, "I'm sorry, Bill. That was nice of you to say. I sincerely appreciate it, especially coming from someone like you."

Wild Bill thanked him for the apology, but couldn't resist asking what he meant by the phrase "someone like me?" Gillie smiled and put on his best wiggle as they walked to the reference desk and asked for a 1953 yearbook. Finally, as the librarian went to get it, Gillie whispered, "I mean someone as rugged and manly as you saying that is a real compliment."

Bill shook his head, and as they took the yearbook, turned and walked toward a table, Bill said, "Gillie, I am not half as rugged as people think I am. You'd be surprised, believe me."

While Gillie and Wild Bill were tenaciously ploughing through the yearbook, Casey and Aaron had located Vicky Martin, who was now Mrs. Red Delaney and lived in nearby Worthville. As Aaron rode through Worthville, he wondered what someone from Casey's background thought as they passed row after row of dilapidated company housing built for the people who worked in the cotton mills for meagre wages. They were paid a pittance, forced to pay rent to the company to live in the squalor of company houses, coerced to buy clothing and food from the company general store and compelled by circumstances to borrow money from the company run savings and loan. These people were the modern equivalent of serfs from the Middle Ages. They were slaves to the privileged class in a country that refused to do anything about the plight of the working men and women. And Casey was part of that privileged class. Heck, even Aaron was on the fringes of the privileged class economically, if not socially. Still, he had empathy for the poor, because he could see that the economic system was set up to make sure that those at the bottom were kept there to serve those at the top. Only a few were allowed to climb the heights of economic prosperity, and that was only done in order to convince those at the bottom that everyone had a chance to succeed. In truth, the cards were always stacked against the poor, because the top slots were reserved for those from the privileged class. Your intelligence was not as important as your lineage in America. Being born with a silver spoon in your mouth was a ticket to success, while the rest got what was left over after the privileged gorged themselves at the table of plenty. And they actually had the nerve to proclaim this system fair.

Casey looked over at Aaron and pensively said, "I know what you are thinking."

Aaron, assuming she had no idea what he was thinking said, "No you don't."

Casey smiled, tilted her head slightly, adjusted in her seat to face Aaron and said, "You are thinking about the appalling conditions in which these people live, and probably thinking that I am from the very class that is responsible."

Aaron, overwhelmed at her perceptiveness, got a grimace on his face as he replied. "Maybe that is what I am thinking. You have to admit the way these people are forced to live is pretty appalling in a nation as wealthy as this one."

"Aaron, I am just as appalled as you are. I live a privileged existence, because I was lucky enough to be born into a wealthy family. I know that I will always have the advantages that others don't, but not all people from wealthy families think they are entitled just because of who their parents are. I am going to devote my life to working with the poor, because I am disgusted by the way this nation ignores their plight and provides the greatest benefits to those at the top of the economic ladder. I displease my father every day, because I am not materialistic and do not intend to practice corporate law. Frankly, I am fed up with my family's crass materialism. I know that life is a struggle for far too many people. I also know that your own father is wealthy, so don't act too high and mighty with me. He is probably wealthier than my father is. The only difference is that he is not as ostentatious as my father. He drives old cars, lives in a modest house, wears clothes off the rack from Jones' Department Store and doesn't belong to the country club or any other of the fancy clubs in town for the elite. You Aaron are part of the privileged class, but simply don't flaunt it."

Aaron could not help but laugh out loud.

Casey laughed too, and said, "you are an alright guy Aaron Adams. You have a heart like no other boy in school. I wouldn't be surprised to see you try and be the American Che Guevara."

Aaron admired Che, and replied with one of his quotes, "I could have been a physician and helped a few thousand people, or I could have been a revolutionary and helped millions."

"You Aaron are rebel-rousing revolutionary in the fine art of irritating, but I am beginning to like it. If you don't irritate people, you aren't accomplishing anything, and believe me; you have irritated a lot of people over the years with your questioning of authority. You truly want to comfort the afflicted, and afflict the comfortable, which is probably what you are going to do with this investigation."

As they drove by the dilapidated housing, a Dickensesque pall fell over the two soft-hearted sojourners into the armpit of agony that was referred to as a mill town. The bridge over Deep River was made of oak and the clattering of the tires over the boards reverberated off the wooden side rails, seemingly playing a melancholy melody of lost hope. They turned to the right after crossing the bridge and to their right on an expansive hillside a few hundred metres down the road there were five long rows of houses in various states of disrepair. They parked at the bottom of the hill and made their way up a wooden walkway on the hillside in search of number 714 Hillside Terrace, where Vicky Martin, now Mrs. Red Delaney lived. Right and left, a multitude of covered walkways led from the main walkway into numerous courts, and the filth and grime on the houses made Casey and Aaron hang their heads in disbelief that people actually were expected to do the back breaking work in a cotton mill and then come home to live in the squalor they saw before them. It was simply inexcusable that a nation of great wealth would actually allow this blight on social justice to exist in the midst of plenty.

As they made their way down Hillside Terrace, they passed through foul pools of stagnant urine and excrement that were bubbling out of a cracked sewer pipe. They turned up the hillside when the walkway curved and had to walk across a board that had been placed over a narrow, coal-black, foul-smelling brook full of debris and refuse. Above the brook were piles of debris around houses packed so close together that a person would have to turn sideways to navigate between them. All the houses were black with soot from the mill and were crumbling relics to the inhumanity of the privileged class that expected their workers to live like animals while they went home to palatial estates high on the mountain overlooking those whom they treated with disdain and contempt.

Aaron looked at Casey and saw that her eyes were tearing up. He reached down, took her hand and gave her a look of reassurance that he, too, was appalled by what they were seeing. These were two people with a heart in a land that simply had too few people who genuinely cared. It was the first time either one of them had ever sat foot in Worthville, and they were overwhelmed by what they were experiencing.

Suddenly, there at the end of the walkway was a monument to greed, 714 Hillside Terrace. The house wasn't just rundown. It was bleak and dreary. It was something that, like the nation that permitted this abomination, was in ruin and decay of the foulest kind. Dark and dreary, it stood in sombre silence, a testament to the evils of an economic system based on avaricious greed. Gazing at its splintered door and a broken window covered with tin foil, Aaron and Casey took deep breaths in preparation for a knock on a door that would lead into a world of despair and abject poverty.

The door swung open and before them stood a young woman who, if she was in different circumstances and could afford some decent clothes and a little makeup, would have been beautiful. The woman had a small baby in her arms and cheerfully greeted them with a gregarious, "hello, may I assist you?"

Aaron said, "Are you Vicky Martin? I mean Vicky Delaney?"

"Yes, I am she," replied the woman, as she shifted the baby from one arm to the other.

Casey said, "We would like to talk to you about the death of Sue Ann McGee, if you have a few minutes."

Nodding her head and motioning them into her home, Vicky replied, "Sure, come in. I think about Sue Ann often. She was my best friend."

They got a glimpse of the dingy rooms. Old frames with cut-outs from magazines decked the walls. The air was putrid and sultry, as the insulation was non existent and the smells from the sewage and debris filtered in and seemed to hang all about. The floors were covered with grimy dust, not from lack of cleaning, but from years of being allowed to pile up so high that it was no longer possible to get it off. Cleaning was probably a waste of time anyway, as you could look down through the slats of the floor and see the ground below. Shadows moved like snakes curling to strike as there was a dark pall that hung over the dimly lit rooms. There was no ceiling, as the beams went right up to the pitched roof. Aaron thought back on the brief few years, as a child, that he had lived in a mill shack while his father was clawing his way out of poverty, but it was nothing like that which he was observing in this den of squalor.

As they sit down on a well-worn sofa, Aaron said, "I am Aaron Adams and this is Casey Felton. We have concluded that Sue Ann McGee's death might not have been an accident, and we are trying to piece together a scenario of just what might have happened that led up to her death. We hope that you might be able to lend us some assistance in our investigation, since you were her best friend in school."

"Best friends, yes we were indeed the very best of friends. You see, we both were probably the poorest two girls in the school, so we just naturally gravitated toward one another. What a sweet girl, who was filled with compassion. She would often encourage me to come to her house to stay, because both my parents were alcoholics who were so boisterous with their drinking and unconcerned about my welfare that they neglected me terribly. On the other hand, Mr. and Mrs. McGee were such loving parents who absolutely doted on Sue Ann. They were really nice to me, too. Frankly, I was very envious of her."

Casey was deeply touched by the loving bond that obviously existed between the two poverty-stricken girls and could not resist offering a comment. "Yes, I can understand how you could be envious. I often find myself envious of others who come from homes where the parents genuinely know how to show love. There is a big difference between love and responsibility. Too many parents just assume that buying things for their children is love. We really need more than material things. We need a depth of understanding and compassion that is often lacking from those who profess to love us. Love is not handing out money. It is not providing material possessions. It is a feeling of warmth, compassion and affection that reaches into your heart; a conscious acceptance of who you are that places no reservations on the pursuit of your dreams."

Aaron, for the first time, realized that Casey was not the care-free, devil-may-care person she always appeared to be. She, too, like Aaron, suffered, on occasion, despair in her relationship with her parents. Sometimes she had pain, but like Aaron, she masked it with gaiety. How little, thought Aaron, does anyone know of the pain so many feel, but do not display. Suddenly, that Joe South song popped into his head:

If I could be you,
And you could be me
For just one hour,
If we could find a way
To get inside
Each other's mind,
If you could see you
Through your eyes
Instead of your ego,
I believe you'd be
Surprised to see
That you've been blind.

Walk a mile in my shoes.
Walk a mile in my shoes.
Hey, before you abuse, criticize and accuse,
Walk a mile in my shoes.

Now your whole world
You see around you
Is just a reflection.
And the law of karma
Says you're gonna reap
Just what you sow, yes you will.

White Meteors and the Ghost of Sue Ann McGee

So unless
You've lived a life of
Total perfection,
You'd better be careful
Of every stone
That you throw.

And yet we spend the day
Throwing stones
At one another
'Cause I don't think
Or wear my hair
The same way you do.

Well I may be
Common people,
But I'm your brother,
And when you strike out
And try to hurt me,
It's a-hurtin' you.

Lord have mercy.
Walk a mile in my shoes.
Walk a mile in my shoes.
Hey, before you abuse, criticize and accuse
Walk a mile in my shoes.

There are people
On reservations,
And out in the ghettos,
And brother there,
But for the grace of God,
Go you and I.

If I only
Had the wings
Of a little angel
Don't you know I'd fly
To the top of the mountain
And then I'd cry:

Walk a mile in my shoes,
Walk a mile in my shoes,
Hey, before you abuse, criticize and accuse
Better walk a mile in my shoes.

As Aaron was going over the lyrics in his head, he looked at Vicky. She was pale and thin. Yet, she had an inherent beauty and elegance about her. The daylight filtered through the tattered sheets that hung in the windows for curtains, almost kissing her knotted and snarled hair as she sat there breast feeding her child, embracing it with deep affection as it suckled for nourishment. One would think that the existence she was forced to call life would have made her heart turn to stone beneath the grinding poverty. Yet, there was a flame of dignity within her. It shone brightly through the filth and depravity of life in a nation that turned a blind eye to the pain and agony in its midst. There was a deep sense of reverence within Aaron for this degraded creature, utterly lost to all sense of shame and humiliation for the sake of survival. Now, she had brought another into a world that would make it a slave to the privileged classes. Birth control was dismissed as immoral by the religious establishment, but which was more immoral, bringing a baby into a life of poverty and deprivation or using a method to avoid the slavery most were destined for?

Aaron, lost in deep thought about the appalling misery of those who toiled for the rich, was snapped back to life when he heard the customary refrain from Casey, "earth to Aaron. Come in Aaron. We can't take up all of Vicky's time. Get to your questions, please."

"Sorry ladies, I was thinking about something else for a moment. Vicky, was there any chance at all that you knew about Sue Ann's pregnancy?"

"No, I was as shocked as everyone else when I heard about it. We were really close, so I just can't figure out why she would not tell me. She would have known the secret was safe with me. Looking back, I realize that I noticed she was putting on weight. It just never occurred to me that she was pregnant. Hey, we joked about sex like most girls, but neither one of us had boyfriends. She especially seemed totally devoid of any interest in boys. She insisted that was not as important as getting an education and somehow getting out of poverty, and then helping her parents."

Aaron, quizzically asked, "Would she have considered an abortion? I know it is illegal, but there are people who perform them."

Vicky, looking surprised that Aaron would mention abortion said, "Yeah, abortion should be legal and a lot of heartache could be avoided, but this is a country where religion has too much sway in government. Everyone in school knew about the woman over on "the hill" who performed abortions. I suppose she is still there. Sue Ann would have had no problems doing it, but she would have had problems getting the money. It was $100 back in those days, and to people like me and Sue Ann, it might as well have been $10,000, because we were so poor that we had trouble getting our hands on 10 cents sometimes."

Aaron leaned forward in his chair and said, "You know the woman's name on the hill?"

"Sure, Sissy Cupcheek. She made a good living taking care of the white girls who got pregnant every year. I suppose she did plenty for her own people, too. It is a shame women have to risk their lives to get an abortion, when it should be legal to walk into the hospital and get one. Then again, poor people would still be kept from getting them, because you can't get medical care in this country without the money to pay for it."

Aaron nodded at Casey, who was one step ahead of him and already had her notepad out and was writing down Sissy Cupcheek's name. Aaron then asked a question that would make Vicky search deep into the recesses of her mind. "So Vicky, think back really hard. Was there absolutely no time that you recall that Sue Ann was seemingly interested in a boy. Anything at all that might be an indication that perhaps she might be meeting someone outside school, someone who might be a key to finding out who the father of her child was. I really believe that is the key to the whole mystery."

Vicky sat in deep, contemplative thought as she took her breast from the baby, buttoned up her blouse and placed him on her shoulder to burp him. Just as he let out a loud burp, and they all laughed, Vicky's eyes actually lit up with a brightness that was like a light bulb being switched on. She blurted out, "Yes, yes, now I remember. Of course, I once saw her after school talking to Rob Waterhouse out by the coal bin. He even reached out and touched her shoulder as they were saying goodbye. He had a strange look on his face, like a loving look. You know, like he really cared for her. Yeah, Robert Waterhouse, and I thought it really strange, because Rob was Eric Parson's best friend. Sue Ann always liked him, but he had pulled a terrible prank on her along with Eric Parson, Mary Lou Hinton and what's her name. Ah, it's on the tip of my tongue, Myra Lewton. I was surprised to see Sue Ann talking to Rob, because she was so disgusted with him a few weeks before when he was part of the prank. She had a crush on him before, but after that she never had anything to do with him. At least I did not think she did, but that day at the coal bin. Yeah, I had forgotten it. You think it is significant?"

Casey, furiously writing down all the names mentioned by Vicky, said, "Anything could be significant, because we have so little to go on right now. What do you think Aaron?"

Aaron, contemplating the significance of Sue Ann speaking to Rob Waterhouse that day, said, "This may be the best clue we have uncovered so far. They were supposed to be enemies, but they were meeting at the coal bin. Is that the same Rob Waterhouse who runs Town and Country Realty?

Vicky chimed in, "The one and only. He went to work there right after university. He married Alicia Anderson, who was also friends with Eric Parson, so close a friend that she and Mary Lou Hinton once had a fist fight in the cafeteria when Mary Lou accused her of dating Eric behind her back. From what I understand, they are still bitter enemies today, but, of course, Mary Lou did not marry Eric, anyway, which is good, because his fidelity is questionable even today. She found someone richer."

Casey offered an interesting comment. "Yeah, tell me about men. They are all circumspect. Fidelity is a foreign word to most of them." Then she looked over at Aaron and smiled as she continued, "present company excepted, of course."

Aaron smiled back, shrugged his shoulders and asked one last question of Vicky. "The day of the funeral, Mrs. McGee said she thinks she saw a cloaked figure near a tree about 100 metres away. Then she saw the figure at the grave, tossing in a flower on the coffin. She was pretty distraught, but seems convinced she saw it."

Vicky never hesitated in her answer. "She saw it. I didn't see anyone at the grave as I left with the crowd, but I did see the figure about 100 metres in the distance by an oak tree. There is no doubt about that. Tall, somewhat thin frame. Couldn't see his face though."

Aaron was beginning to make connections. "So, would you say his frame was very similar to that of Rob Waterhouse?"

Again, that light went on in Vicky's eyes. "Yeah, yeah, it was a lot like him in stature."

Casey, amazed at Aaron's investigative powers, looked at him in awe. Aaron, felt pretty good about himself, too. He winked at Casey and began to get up. "Vicky, you have really been helpful. We will keep you posted on what we find out. We are determined to get to the truth about what really happened."

Vicky got up, cradled the baby in her arms and said, "Sue Ann deserved so much better. I failed to get out of poverty. I fell into the same trap as my parents, but even with a baby, I think Sue Ann would have made it. She was just too determined to fail. She was going to do whatever it took to get through university and make a real life for herself.

Casey walked over to Vicky, looked down at the baby and said, "You may not be rich in money Vicky, but you have something that is worth more than money. I can tell you are a good mother, and this baby is going to grow up with love. There are far too many children who grow up with material things, but never know what it is like to be truly loved. Don't give up on yourself."

Vicky was obviously touched by what Casey said. She smiled up at her and proudly replied, "My husband is at night school now. He is getting his electrician's certificate, soon. Once he does, he is quitting the mill and going to work for a company in Greensboro that is unionized, so he will be making a decent wage. Then, I am going to secretarial school, so that when the baby is in school, I can go to work. We are not going to be defeated like so many others by the unfair system of servitude that traps far too many. We are smart enough to have only one child, because we know it is unfair to bring children into a world where most will be nothing but slaves to the ruling class."

Aaron and Casey thanked Vicky for her time, and they walked out of the dilapidated shack down to the car at the bottom of the hill. Still depressed by the squalor, the two were mostly silent as they left behind the misery that trapped so many in the quagmire of despair. Aaron's four wheeled chariot of chrome and steel bore them through the slums of anguish and dashed hopes, where the muffled cries for help were ignored by a society that had lost its moral compass.

How many hopeless cries, thought Aaron, are stilled by a society that wants to enslave most of its citizens to the drudgery of a life on the outside looking in? Sue Ann McGee was one of those faceless millions who were discarded by a society with no heart or soul. Ah, but Sue Ann had two champions who were in search of justice. Forgotten woman, gloomy ghost; these two were going to minister to her sorrow and put their warm arms around her in the darkness of her despair and then Sue Ann would know truth's sanctity.

CHAPTER 6
EMBRACE US ALL IN THE END

I am told the pain
will ease with time.
That I will think
of her without a tear.
But that is impossible,
because I need her here.
Our love was interrupted
by something evil and foul.
Oh, the cold ground,
it embraces her now.

Gillie and Wild Bill were anxiously awaiting the arrival of Casey and Aaron, sitting on Casey's steps under the porch light that her father had unceremoniously turned on as he told them to wait outside for the return of his daughter and the young man whom he thought was absolutely beneath her. Now, in addition to Aaron Adams, there was a ruffian dressed like a hillbilly sitting on Mr. Felton's porch next to a gay blade attired like he was a court jester in 17th century France, waiting to see his daughter who was rapidly incurring his wrath as she obviously did not care what the neighbours thought about the cast of characters that she was now calling friends. This would have to cease!

Aaron and Casey were surprised to see the two waiting there for them. As they pulled up, the boys leaped from their perches and came over to the driver's side window beaming with smiles and shouting, "wait until you hear what we found. You won't believe it. You won't!"

Gillie placed his left hand on Wild Bill's shoulder and said, "Go ahead Wild Bill. You tell them about it."

Bill was so excited his words came out like bullets from a machine gun, so rapid fire that they were impossible to comprehend. Aaron said, "slow down, Bill, Slow down and let's hear it from the beginning."

"OK Aaron, we were pouring over every word, every picture, and we thought that we simply had not found anything that would be of value. Then, we decided to look in the back of the book also. You know the pages where all the ads are. Nobody reads them. The pages are just used by people writing in each others' yearbooks. You know, where they put all that stupid stuff saying how you will succeed. How nice you are. Stuff that is mostly lies. Anyway, there was an ad for the Sunset Theatre, and there was a picture of the front of the theatre. There's a line of people going in, and you can see their profiles just a bit. We squint and stare, even go to get a magnifying glass and there is Sue Ann McGee, we know it was her, walking in through the double doors. Behind her is Rob Waterhouse. But get this. We look really close with the magnifying glass and she has her hand behind her back and Waterhouse seems to be stroking it with his index finger. I'm telling you, there was something up between those two. Anyway, then we go to the theatre and talk to Mr. Broughton, you know, the manager. We ask when that picture was taken. He is so nice. He goes through his photo files and there it is. It was taken the very night before Sue Ann McGee had her accident."

Gillie interjected, "we did good, uh, Aaron?"

Aaron, nodding his head, said, "You boys did excellent. Get in the back seat and we'll share with you what we found out."

Before long, Casey's father could be seen peeking through the living room window at the four of them. Shaking her head, Casey said, "I'll see you guys tomorrow. I better go in before my dad has a heart attack."

Aaron looked at her with determination. "He better get used to us. You are now part of the upper echelon of Asheboro society."

Casey, laughing as Wild Bill got out of the back seat to take her place in the front seat said, "I've been waiting all my life for this boys. I have finally arrived."

The three boys laughed heartily as they drove off, Casey waving while Aaron's car belched blue smoke as it careened around the huge circular driveway, heading toward the bronze gate that led onto the road in front of Casey's house. She shouted at him, "Pick me up tomorrow morning."

The next day, Aaron and Casey were the talk of the school, as no one could figure out why they had suddenly become a pair. Then, there was Gillie and Wild Bill. Talk about a pair! No one dared make fun of Wild Bill for fear that he would pulverize them into oblivion. As for Gillie, it seemed that the teasing he had endured for years had finally subsided. Unfortunately, it was not out of new found respect for him or acceptance of his lifestyle, but out of fear that his new found friend, Wild Bill, might be offended. Fear can be used effectively, as the USA had proved for years by making the populace fearful of an immanent communist takeover of the world. It kept the citizens in line, saluting the flag, pledging allegiance and accepting repression all in the name of defending freedom. This fear would lead to a huge debacle in Vietnam, and many years later it would be utilized to justify a needless war in Iraq by a buffoonish President and his henchmen who would pass all kinds of freedom curtailing laws in the name of national security. Fear drives people to line up to put shackles on their own ankles. Patriotism, as used by American politicians, was nothing more than a refuge for scoundrels. In the case of Wild Bill and Gillie, fear kept timid people at bay. Ironically, that fear was generally unfounded, because Wild Bill had never been in but a few fights, and they were more skirmishes than fights, except that one with Aaron. That one was a donnybrook that people still talked about. However, most of the talk was about how Aaron refused to quit and Wild Bill finally just walked away in frustration from hitting him so much.

That day, Aaron and Casey had to meet Gillie and Wild Bill in the football stadium at noon to discuss their plans for the day's investigations. They were running late, so they cut through the gym and headed down the infamous corridor to take the back door out to the stadium. Just as they got to the locker room door, for some reason they stopped as if expecting something to occur. The corridor was dark, and as customary, there was that cold that permeated all about, seeming to chill not just the body, but the soul. Casey reached down and took Aaron's hand.

Casey's pretty face was quite pale over the jeopardy of the situation, and it then slowly flushed up. Her large dark eyes flashed fire, and her trim little figure, so nicely fitted into a tight-fitting skirt, quivered all over with excitement from the mysterious force that seemed to be luring the two of them to open the door and walk into the locker room.

They knew not why, but there was some peculiar grace luring Aaron's left hand to turn the knob. Some forms, though bright in lustrous intent, no mortal man or woman can resist. These two were drawn inexplicably to the darkness of the locker room that was rarely used. The dark seemed to engulf the two as the door quietly closed behind them. Yet, they were unafraid, though Casey tightly gripped Aaron's hand, more out of anticipatory expectation than fear. They made no attempt to turn on the light. They simply made their way forward in the darkness, moving tentatively, but with no trepidation, toward the shower stalls behind the large tile wall. Then the light came on in the showers and a lone shower could be heard as steam began to rise toward the ceiling. Some forms, though fearful, no mortal man can resist. These two intrepid sojourners into the unknown could see the form of a woman taking shape in the steam as they stood there in awe.

Beauty and anguish walk hand-in-hand on the downward slope of death, peopling the hallowed dark like burning stars blazing their last light. In that ghostly image forming above them was a moan of anguish that scorched the hearts of Aaron and Casey. They heard sounds of insult, shame and wrong that trumpeted a war of pain.

The spectre before them was shrunken with pain, but the intense, agonizing, soulful moans indicated a desire, an incredibly burning desire to communicate. The entity seemed to be beguiling them from the deep, forlorn and lonely grave. The sinews no longer held the flesh and bones together; those had perished in the earth that encompassed her in the nearby cemetery as the fierceness of the consuming fire of death enveloped her in the trap of eternal darkness. But the soul, the soul flitted away in search of peace, as though it was in nightmarish pursuit of those who had tormented and damned her in life. Sue Ann McGee had perished without whispers and grey clouds sadly enveloped her spirit as dark oceans of despair embraced her. Unfinished business punctuated by a violent death was, without a doubt, the motive for the ghostly visitation.

Casey and Aaron stood quietly, almost reverentially, as the steamy figure bounced about, then disappeared. The lone running shower shut off and they instinctively looked at the mirror above the middle wash basin. Once again, there was writing on the steam-laden mirror. This time it was more than one word. The words were rapidly dissipating, as they ran down the mirror. The disappearing moisture was a fading testament to the misery suffered by Sue Ann McGee before her final plunge into oblivion. The words were gone now, but Casey and Aaron stood staring at one another, enthralled and mesmerized by what they had just witnessed. Neither had ever put any credence in things that could not be physically explained. Miracles were just unexplained events that had no basis in fact and were nothing more than fairy tales, but now they were faced with ghostly apparitions that defied explanation – and the words, the words on the mirror were branded into their minds.

THEY KILLED ME!

It was no longer a lone killer. It was "they." Yes, the word "they" was there. There was more than one person involved.

Not wanting to unduly alarm Gillie and Wild Bill, Casey and Aaron did not mention the episode in the locker room. Rather, they gave them the job of gathering all the background information they could on Rob Waterhouse and Eric Parson from their high school days to the present. Meanwhile, Casey and Aaron were going to visit Mary Lou Hinton, who now was married and living in nearby Greensboro's Everly Estates, the crème-de-la-crème of North Carolina's affluent housing developments.

How the now 27 year old Mary Lou Hinton got to Everly Estates fascinated both Casey and Aaron. A little preliminary research revealed that Mary Lou, during her sophomore year at the University of North Carolina had decided not to wait on her beloved Eric while he was away at another university. One weekend, she went home with a girlfriend whose father was none other than Billy Hindle, the former New York Yankee first baseman who had retired with his wife and two children to Greensboro, where he bought two car dealerships. Only two months after meeting the then 19 year old Mary Lou Hinton, the 44 year old Hindle had unceremoniously dumped his wife, and Mary Lou had suddenly quit school and moved into the stately mansion. A few months later they were married, and now Mary Lou was part of Greensboro high society.

As they drove into Everly Estates, they noticed the road was made of stone, rather than asphalt. Suddenly, a large brick guardhouse loomed in the distance and Aaron thought to himself that it was just another example of the rich walling themselves off from the real people. They had to be protected from the riff-raff that might offend their sensibilities. At the guardhouse, a man of perhaps 60 stepped out and asked whom they were there to see? Aaron said, "Mrs. William Hindle, but she is not expecting us. We are Aaron Adams and Casey Felton from Asheboro."

The guard said, "I will call her to see if you can come in." Then, he turned and walked back inside the guardhouse. Casey looked at Aaron and shook her head, smiled and then grimaced.

Aaron, almost laughing, said, "So, you are from Asheboro high society. What you think of high society in Greensboro?"

Casey shook her head and replied, "These are ostentatious jerks who are even more arrogant than my dad could ever be. I thought where we lived was disgusting. This is absolutely ghastly and a prime example of what is wrong with this country. No one should be allowed to live like this when we have kids going to bed hungry at night."

Each day Aaron spent with Casey he gained more respect for her. She saw the despicableness of the rich thinking they were entitled to a life of arrogant luxury while most people toiled for meagre wages in the offices, factories and fields of despair. Like Aaron, she saw this kind of living as an affront to human dignity.

The guard stepped out and said, "She doesn't know you, so I am afraid you will have to turn around and leave."

Aaron, never one to bow before arrogance, indignantly barked, "Get back on the phone you rent-a-cop protector of the rich and tell her that she can either see us or we will go down to the car dealership to see her husband. We are here to discuss the murder of Sue Ann McGee and her complacency in said murder. Use those exact words."

The guard, not used to being talked to in that manner by someone of dubious breeding and a teenager, at that, reached down and put his hand on the pistol that was in a holster on his hip, while staring menacingly at Aaron.

Aaron, not intimidated, said, "you going to use that thing to protect your arrogant bosses, or are you going to do as I ask? Frankly, I think going to jail for murdering two teenagers to protect the jerks who live here is pretty stupid."

The guard turned, went back inside for a short time and emerged with a grim look on his face. "She says to come on up. Turn right inside the gate and take that road all the way to the end of the cul-de-sac. The Hindle house is the big colonial. It has a circular drive in the front. You and me are going to meet in another place at another time, and I will teach you some manners."

As he pulled off, Aaron said, "Looking forward to it."

Casey grinned, reached over and touched Aaron's arm. "You think you are tough. Anybody ever challenge you?"

Aaron replied, "Sure! Once Wild Bill did and I wore his fists out by making him hit me so many times. Left me alone after that, because he didn't want to tear up his hands breaking my face."

Casey laughed until they reached the end of the cul-de-sac. Then she was awe-struck. There, standing like a monument to excess, was the most enormous house either one of them had ever seen. Well, maybe besides the Biltmore mansion in Asheville that they toured once on a school field trip.

Money can buy many of things in America, but one of the most important things it bought for those who worshipped at the exalted altar of greed was envy. Making others envy you was at the very core of what rich people needed to gratify their gargantuan egos. This house was an incredibly vivid statement of audacious arrogance, and arrogance was what most rich people were all about. The world's governments, even those that professed more equality than America, where capitalism was worshipped like a God, were in service to the rich and their corporations that raped, plundered and destroyed the planet to satisfy the insatiable desire for more and more.

J. Wayne Frye

Driving up the circular cobblestone driveway toward the magnificent finely polished stone edifice, with its eight bright while marble Corinthian columns, the two teenagers were struck with the absurd ostentatious display of wealth in a land filled with poverty and inequality of opportunity. This was an abomination of monumental magnitude.

Aaron's 1952 Buick bellowed blue smoke out the exhaust as it belched its way up the driveway, coming to a squeaking halt in front of the magnificent Italian marble steps that wound down from the impressive gold inlaid entry doors. Aaron got out, went around to the other side of the car and opened the door for Casey who glided out of the old automobile as if she was getting out of a Rolls Royce. She took Aaron's arm, smiled at him and they gracefully walked up the marble steps. Aaron could not resist looking back at his pile-of-junk car and thinking that the cobblestone driveway would be filled with oil when he left, because the car was like a sieve when it came to oil. Yeah, thought Aaron, the Hindle's would really be upset when they saw all the oil on the expensive cobblestones that, no doubt, made them burst with pride when all their friends and family drove up on them to their mansion for Champaign and caviar.

Casey looked at him, grinned, tilted her head and said, "I know what you are thinking. You are a scoundrel, Aaron Adams. You can't wait to drive down that expensive cobblestone driveway and leave a trail of oil behind you. It is your way of punishing them for their flamboyantly extravagant lifestyle. You are a naughty boy."

Aaron, sensing an opening, replied, "Casey, give me half a chance, and I will show you what a naughty boy I can really be."

Casey, used to boys trying to be naughty with her, replied, "I have been handling naughty boys all my life, Aaron. Believe me, I can handle you."

As they got to the door, Aaron whispered softly, "I think I am breaking you down, Casey. You are beginning to realize what a nice guy I am. You are considering giving me a chance."

Casey, not missing a beat, said, "Ring the bell, Mr. Modesty."

Aaron felt so good just being near her. It was almost as if he owed a debt of gratitude to the ghost of Sue Ann McGee for making it all possible.

The door was not just opened; it was grandly swirled inward in a sweeping motion while the immaculately attired butler stepped into the entryway with his tall, robust, masculine frame blocking the two interlopers from entering the house. He stood there, shoulders thrown back, chest puffed out and a look of utter disdain on his face for the two scruffily dressed unworthy young people who had the audacity to ask to see someone of Mrs. Hindle's stature. He said in a gruff manner, "Madam will see you in the drawing room." Then he looked down at their feet, rolled his eyes and pointed to the floor mat at the threshold of the doorway. "You may wipe your feet there, please."

Aaron, as always, resented arrogance on the part of anyone. He very flippantly said, "You sure you don't want us to take off our shoes. I washed my feet really well this morning."

The butler raised his chin, rolled his eyes again and pointed toward the room to their right as he snobbishly said, "Follow me, please."

Walking into the luxurious drawing room was an experience that dazzled the eyes. The most prominent feature was a huge gold chandelier with shimmering crystal that reflected the light from the two monstrously large windows that looked out into a glass roofed atrium filled with exotic birds. The chirping sounds were completely muffled by the thick leaded Tiffany glass, and sitting there on a plush, brocade Versailles sofa beneath the chandelier was an immaculately attired Mary Lou Hinton, her legs crossed and a look of defiant arrogance on her face as she looked up at the butler and said, "thank you James. That will be all."

Mary Lou pointed at a love seat by the windows and said, "You may sit down. Please get to the point as quickly as possible, as I am very busy this afternoon. I believe you made some ridiculous statement about Sue Ann McGee being murdered. I am afraid that I am completely in the dark about that. I was there when she fell from the grappling rope. It was obviously an accident."

Aaron could not help but notice her shapely, muscular calves as she shifted in her seat, crossing and uncrossing her legs. Her dress was hiked up just high enough for Aaron to get a glimpse of her smooth, equally shapely thighs. Her body hugging dress had just the right amount of cleavage to accentuate her breasts that seemed to be fighting for freedom from the garment.

Casey gave Aaron a perplexed look, as he was concentrating on Mary Lou's sexiness rather than on the real reason they were there. Typical of a teenage boy thought Casey. Then she reflected a bit and thought to herself that it was typical of all men, period. Men were such idiots! She took a deep breath and got a scent of Mary Lou's lilac scented perfume.

So, Casey decided she would have to start the questioning until Aaron could regain his composure. "Mrs. Hinton, you had a romantic relationship with Eric?"

Shrugging her shoulders, Mary Lou disdainfully replied. "Yes, I was a fool at the time. I was one of many girls he was using. He even went behind my back with my best friend. Well, I thought she was my best friend, Alicia Anderson."

Casey looked at Aaron and continued. "And, you were involved in a running feud with Eric against Sue Ann McGee?"

"We were. What's so unusual about that? Adolescents are prone to be spiteful."

Aaron, now more composed, said, "Spite is one thing. Murder is another."

Mary Lou straightened up, leaned forward slightly and stridently said, "I told you. The bitch died in an acccidnt."

Now, Aaron was ready to bore in hard. "That's right. You thought she was a bitch, because she stood up to Eric's arrogance. That is something you and him both were not used to, were you?"

"Arrogance? What do you mean arrogance? We were just sitting in the car and that low-life white trash decided to call Eric a jerk for no reason at all."

Aaron was going to enjoy this. "That is not the way I heard it. It appears the jerks were you, Eric and the rest of your crowd who took offence when anyone dared stand up to your arrogance. Just because you are from a rich family doesn't make you any better than the low-life white trash you have so much contempt for. The real trash in this world is those who think money, power and position makes them better than others."

Mary Lou stood up and said, "Get out of my house. You don't come in here and talk to me like that!"

Casey, realizing the intent of Aaron's outburst was to play a psychological game, tried to calm down Mary Lou. "We are sorry Mrs. Hinton, please; there is no need to get upset." She then turned to Aaron and said, "you are sorry aren't you Aaron?"

Aaron, now pleased that he had done exactly as he intended, make Casey the good guy as a result of his tirade, meekly replied, "Yes, I am terribly sorry. My behaviour was inappropriate Mrs. Hinton. You were nice enough to see us. I don't have the tack Casey does."

Mary Lou, smugly replied, "Apology accepted, go on with your questions, but make it quick."

Casey, taking the cue from Aaron, asked very politely, "Is there any chance it could not have been an accident, anything at all that might have aroused your suspicion before or after Sue Ann fell?"

Sitting back down, and crossing her legs again. This time slowly and methodically to purposefully give the youthful, hormonally driven young Aaron the full view of her alluring shapeliness as a way to tease and tantalize him, Mary Lou actually seemed more interested in sharing information. "Well, there was one incident that I have thought about over the years. I didn't think much of it at the time, but now that you seem so intent that it wasn't an accident, maybe it is significant."

Casey interjected, "please, tell us about it."

Mary Lou now almost seemed eager to share the information. "A few weeks before Sue Ann's death, Eric and I were at the country club dance together. As usual, Eric's dad asked me to dance. He was a dirty old man who was always looking at me and constantly trying to get me alone, away from Eric. I knew what he was up to. What all men are up to?" She then gave Aaron a disdainful look and continued. "Anyway, as Mr. Parson and I were dancing, he asked me about the long ago incident with Sue Ann McGee. I shared the information, but then he said something really funny. Well, not funny in a comical sense, funny in the sense of being so unusual. It was something that just came out of nowhere."

Aaron, no longer distracted by the alluring nature of Mary Lou, said, "What was it?"

"It was a question. He asked if Sue Ann was in my PE class. It didn't mean much at the time, but over the years, I have thought about it. You see, a week later, Sue Ann died from the fall in PE class."

Casey and Aaron looked at each other. This was an interesting development that was not expected. Then, Aaron leaned forward, looked directly at Mary Lou and said, "I am not trying to be crude Mary Lou, but I need to ask this. Was Eric always faithful to you?"

Mary Lou let out a subdued laugh. "Faithful, you have to be kidding. He didn't know the meaning of the word."

"Do you have any idea of who he might have been unfaithful with?

"You name them. He probably tried to make it with 'um. Of course, Alicia and I had a big fight over her dalliance with him and that was the end of our so-called friendship. Eric wound up marrying some rich society woman from Charlotte handpicked by his father. His father always controlled him. In fact, he is still controlling him even today from what I hear. Eric has absolutely no backbone when it comes to his father. Whatever his father says do, Eric does without question."

Then, Aaron asked a question that surprised Mary Lou and Casey both. "Any chance he was ever interested in Sue Ann McGee? She was a pretty attractive girl."

Mary Lou got a contemplative look as a silence fell upon the room. She stared off into space, seemingly in deep, thoughtful reflection.

Aaron was about to break the silence when Mary Lou blurted out. "Yeah, I think maybe he was. I caught him sneaking glances at her several times. He always covered it up by making some snide remark about her, but, yeah. Yeah, I think he may have been interested in her."

Casey looked at Aaron and glanced at her watch, signalling that maybe they should be leaving before Mr. Hindle came home.

Aaron thanked Mary Lou as he got a last whiff of her provocative smelling perfume, and as he and Casey got up to leave, she surprised them both when she said, "I know what you think of me. Believe me, I know what I am. I will lose my looks some day, and I will have nothing. That is all I have, nothing else."

Aaron, still not particularly caring for her, decided to leave on a good note. "Don't sell yourself short. You would be surprised what you might be if you really tried. There is a lot more to life than a luxurious house, expensive cars, fancy clothes and a wad of green. Think about it. We all, regardless of our station in life, are headed for the same place Sue Ann McGee is – the cold ground will embrace us all in the end.

CHAPTER 7
THIS WAS GILLIE"S FINEST HOUR

How strangely blind is prejudice, humanity's greatest foe!
It never fails to see wrong but naught of good can know.
'Tis blind to all that's lofty, to truth it is opposed.
Degrading things will open eyes,
but the good keep them closed.
How cruel is prejudice! How wicked is the tongue!
The evils reign supremely there, the bad is ever sung.
It is man's greatest curse, it festers like an open sore.
It slowly saps precious life, it is poison to the core.

Winding down the cobblestone drive with the blue exhaust smoke flowing behind them like a signal of disdain, Aaron and Casey could only look at one another in disbelief. They shook their heads at the evil of a society that allowed so few to accumulate so much, while the vast majority begged for crumbs from the tables of plenty set for those at the top. No country is truly free when it allows those at the top of the economic ladder to control those beneath them. Real freedom in America was reserved for those who could afford it. Even medical care and justice came with a price tag in America. It was a sad state of affairs that the majority of the brainwashed population supported in the misplaced belief that everyone had a shot at making it, when in truth; those born into privilege always got the best shot at everything. Casey broke the silence as they sailed by the gate, Aaron dismissively waving at the guard. "Aaron, I know it seems ridiculous, but I actually feel sorry for Mary Lou. She sold herself to the highest bidder. I don't think she is all that happy."

Aaron, always the philosopher, said, "She may indeed be unhappy, but if you are going to be unhappy anyway, it is better to be happy with money than without."

The two of them laughed and continued their drive back to Asheboro, where the following day, the investigation would take a dramatic turn, courtesy of Gillie and Wild Bill who were, at that very moment, making a discovery that would somewhat alter the trail of suspicion.

Trusted with doing research on Rob Waterhouse and Eric Parson, Gillie and Wild Bill had poured over all kinds of materials in both the school and town library, much to the chagrin of the librarians in both facilities, who acted offended that two boys of dubious intent were so interested in past history. Furthermore, both librarians had always been dismissive of Gillie, as they did not like the way he flaunted his lifestyle. The town librarian, Mrs. Crutchfield, who was also the church choir director, would not even hand Gillie the materials, because as she had told one of her co-workers, "I do not want to be near that abomination to decency. He will one day burn in the fires of hell for the sin of homosexuality."

She threw the materials in front of him, as if his mere touch would be like acknowledging the presence of the devil himself. As she tossed down the April 1953 editions of the *Randolph Picayune* newspaper in front of Gillie, Wild Bill, placing his left hand on Gillie's right shoulder, looked up at her and said, "Mrs. Crutchfield, you are a public servant, and Gillie here is part of the public. You need to show a little more respect for the children of those who pay your salary."

She huffed a bit, turned and walked away as she mumbled something, no doubt, derogatory, under her breath.

Gillie, extremely impressed with Wild Bill's defence of him, uttered, "Thank you, Bill. That was nice of you."

Wild Bill shrugged his shoulders, gave Gillie a stern look and replied, "Hey, don't think I want a date or something. It's no big deal."

Gillie smiled and said, "It's no big deal to you, but it is a big deal to me. Outside of Aaron Adams, no male has ever been my friend in school. Of course, out of school, some of them sneak around and flirt with me, but they aren't brave enough to be seen with me in school."

Wild Bill, flippantly barked as he smiled broadly, "Don't get the idea I am your friend."

Gillie smiled back and said, "hey big boy. I know you are my friend. In fact, you may break down yet and ask me for a date."

Bill disdainfully shook his head and said, "Get to work you big flirt. That's about as likely to happen as Richard Nixon ever being elected President."

The two of them judiciously poured over the newspaper clippings, and right on the front page of one newspaper was a story about the MGM lion appearing at the Sunset Theatre. That was interesting reading, looking at people standing near it and having their photographs taken, but a closer look with the magnifying glass revealed another real find in the background. There was Sue Ann McGee in the photo, standing among the crowd staring at the lion which was on a leash, and to her left was none other than Rob Waterhouse, who seemed to be trying really hard to ignore the fact that she was next to him. The charade simply wasn't working though, because you could see that Rob was glancing over at her out of the corner of his right eye. Likewise, she was glancing at him with her left eye, and the looks on their faces were intense. So intense were the looks that one could not help but realize that these two were intensely aware of each other's presence. In fact, were they meeting at the movies secretly? Were they just making it appear that they were not together?

As Wild Bill started to place down the magnifying glass, Gillie reached out and touched his hand. Wild Bill gave him a stern look of disapproval, but Gillie said, "No, no, don't get all discombobulated. Look, take the magnifying class and look six people over from the right of Sue Ann, to your left of course. Go back four rows and tell me who that is standing there staring at Sue Ann and Rob. Go ahead; we have seen that face in the trophy case at school and the yearbook from 1953. Look!"

Wild Bill raised the magnifying glass and there was a real shocker. Yes, standing there was none other than Eric Parson. Eric Parson was at the Sunset Theatre, too. All three of them were there at the same time.

Excited with their find at a time when libraries had no copying machines, they recorded the date of the newspaper, and the next day took Aaron and Casey to the library to show them what they had found. Needless to say, Mrs. Crutchfield was less than thrilled.

The four of them walked to Hop's after going over the newspaper photo. There, with her customary good cheer was Lauralee, although she did seem a bit surprised to see Wild Bill and Gillie together. Casey and Aaron with Gillie would have made sense, as they were always, like her, opened minded and accepting, but Wild Bill? Wild Bill was a shock.

They all sat in the same back booth that Aaron had shared with Casey on what he thought, at the time, was a date. In fact, with Casey sitting beside him, he was going back over that day, and how it was the beginning of a new chapter in their relationship. It still wasn't the romantic relationship he desired, but it was a start. Just sitting next to her, he could feel her warmth. He so desperately wanted to reach down and take her hand, but he felt she might rebuke him; consequently, he restrained himself and plunged right into what the significance of the photo was by asking, "so, were they all three aware of each other being there? Asheboro was an even smaller town then than now. Any reasonable person could tell by the eyes that Sue Ann and Rob were certainly aware of each others presence. What do you guys think?"

Casey said, "They were sweethearts. Two people who weren't supposed to care for each other were sweethearts. Sue Ann and Rob were meeting at the theatre. My guess is that they went in separately, but probably sneaked up into the back of the balcony where it is super dark. It is so dark up there that you can't see your hand in front of your face. They watched the movie together." Then she let out a little giggle and continued, "Probably necking in the pitch darkness."

Gillie couldn't resist interjecting. "Yeah, I've always wanted to go up there, but never got the nerve!"

Wild Bill looked at him disgustingly and said, "This isn't about you, pervert. It's about Sue Ann McGee and Rob Waterhouse being sweethearts when everyone thought they were supposed to be enemies. Sometimes sweethearts have a tendency to do things that can lead to pregnancy."

Aaron then offered his usual intuitive deductive reasoning. "Yeah, that is true, and that certainly could have happened between the two of them, but dates are important. We need to deduce how long the relationship was going on before the pregnancy to decide if the baby was Rob's, and now we have another element thrown into the mix. Eric Parson apparently knew what was going on between them. What part could he have played in the whole thing?"

Casey, intrigued by the new developments said, "OK, Aaron and I will visit Rob and Eric. Maybe you two should not go, because we don't want to overpower them with a show of force. You two have done a remarkable job, absolutely remarkable."

Gillie seemed to be really pleased with himself and asked, "So, we think Sue Ann's death was not an accident, but just where is all this leading?"

Aaron replied, "It is leading to a murderous plot involving, in my opinion, more than one person. There are some insidious elements connected to this whole affair, and my guess is that everything revolves around the pregnancy of Sue Ann. After all, getting pregnant when you are unmarried is considered abominable by the moralists who spend more time pointing the finger of condemnation than reaching out with the hand of compassion. Abortion is illegal, so girls are not allowed to control their own bodies. The results for those who decide to abort are often catastrophic, because they can't go to a doctor for the procedure. Over on the Hill is a woman named Sissy Cupcheek, who performs abortions for people with a bit of green. I am going to see her, because my guess is that she might have been approached about an abortion for Sue Ann, if not by Sue Ann herself, perhaps by the father of the baby. There is not only a murderer on the loose; there are other people who were culpable in the crime. This is a great little town with some terrific people living in it, but like all good places, there are those who think they are above the law and can get away with anything because of wealth and power. I intend to spend my life comforting the afflicted and afflicting the comfortable. I have a feeling some really powerful people are going to be exposed. That is what I live for, watching those who think they are above the normal rules of society, because of who they are, being brought down from their lofty perches. The arrogance of the rich and powerful makes me cringe with indignation.

Casey interjected, "My Aaron, a lover of the common man like his hero, Che Guevara said, "*If you tremble with indignation at every injustice, then you are a comrade of mine.* You borrow his rhetoric without proper citation and Miss Powell will rake you over the coals."

Aaron replied sarcastically, "Per Miss Powell's instructions, when paraphrasing, a reference citation is not mandatory, Miss Know-it-all Casey Felton, who just happens to be from the privileged class that my hero Che had so much disdain for."

Casey, always enjoying the banter with Aaron continued. "I may be from the privileged class, but that is not my fault. You can blame my parents for that. Don't judge all for the actions of a few."

Aaron, never one to give on social issues, replied, "You, I don't judge, because I know you carry a genuine soft spot in your heart for the working men and women of the world, but you are wrong about the actions of the few. It is the actions of the majority of rich people that are repugnant. Rich people like you are, unfortunately, in the minority."

Gillie looked at Wild Bill and said, "Yeah, Aaron's dad is rich but doesn't act like it. Casey's dad is rich and does act like it. On the other hand, we are the only two at this table who can speak with authority on being poor, because we really are poor. We know what it is like to watch parents struggle day-to-day just to put food on the table."

Casey offered a gem of wisdom: "Gillie, you and Wild Bill are only poor in material things. You are rich in the things that count."

Gillie and Wild Bill both felt genuine respect in Casey's remark. She and Aaron were both special when it came to being accepting and non-judgemental. They were the only two who had really been openly friendly with Gillie, and now Wild Bill, who had always been feared more than respected, also felt their warmth and concern. How ionic that it took the murder of Sue Ann McGee for them all to find one another.

Ever the realist, Wild Bill said, "Let's get off this philosophical malarkey and get down to business. We have a murder to solve, because no one else but us is interested, because the one killed was poor, and in this town and in this country, the poor simply don't get the justice they deserve."

The group broke up after Aaron stated that he planned to visit Sissy Cupcheek the following afternoon to see what information he could glean from her. At school that day, Willie Simpson, an arrogant moralistic hypocrite who was always preaching to others about the sinfulness of the modern world and how the wrath of God would be poured out among the heathens, was entering the boys' bathroom with some friends when Gillie got to the door at the same time. Willie, defiantly pushed him aside and said, "You need to use the girl's bathroom. This is the man's bathroom, and you are no man."

Gillie, a young man who was tired of the years of harassment, decided for one of the few times in his life to make a stand against bigotry and judgmental arrogance. He looked Willie in the face and said, "Then if it is a men's room, I suppose you won't be going in either."

That opened up a torrent of vindictive rhetoric from Willie, who was not used to having his superior moral attitudes challenged. "You dirty little queer. You are an affront to God and the Good Book. When you are burning in hell for your abominations, I will be dancing in heaven with Jesus and his angels."

Gillie was not about to back down now. He puffed out his chest and stood on his toes to appear taller, which still made him look puny compared to the muscular and tall Willie Simpson, and said, "Well, if jerks like you are going to be in heaven, I'd rather be in hell."

By then, a large crowd had gathered and most people laughed at Gillie's remark, which only further enraged Willie, who suddenly drew back his right hand in preparation to deliver a blow that would have, no doubt, if it connected, have sent Gillie to the Pearly Gates to meet St. Peter, who would instantly dispatch him to hell for his blatant homosexuality. Fortunately, standing behind Willie was Wild Bill McCloud, who reached out and took hold of Willie's hand and said, "I really don't think you want to do that, Willie."

Willie turned to face the slightly shorter Wild Bill and said, "You standing up for this queer? You take the side of someone who is offensive to God, and you will wind up in hell with him."

Bill smiled and said, "Willie, I'll let God make those decisions, not you. I don't recall reading anywhere that he made you the judge of what is moral and immoral. You live your life and let Gillie live his."

J. Wayne Frye

Suddenly, a small group of students actually started to vigorously applaud Wild Bill's statement. Willie, now fearful of Wild Bill, lowered his head, turned and aggressively pushed his way through the crowd as Gillie shouted after him, "Headed toward the girls' bathroom, Willie?"

Wild Bill gave Gillie a stern look and said, "Don't push your luck Gillie. I am not always going to be around to back you up. And believe me, your skinny self is absolutely no match for most of the boys in this school."

Wild Bill walked away as Gillie stuck out his chest and proudly pushed open the door to the boys' bathroom, basking in his new found pride. Several boys patted him on the back as they passed by him, one saying, "It's about time someone stood up to that bombastic Bible-thumping hypocrite."

That was a momentous day that would forever shine in Gillie's memory. Yes, his friend had rescued him, but Gillie had also taken a stand against injustice. This was nothing short of a monumental occurrence, especially in the Bible Belt of America where African Americans were still being denied the right to vote and, as for gays, the very word was an abomination in the south. It was 1963, and what had just occurred was unheard of at the time. That was a day when some "White Meteors" at the school took a bold stand against hate and bigotry based on sexual orientation. Gillie thought to himself, as a few of the boys walked down the hall with him toward class, that something had changed at the school and it had all started when he hooked up with Aaron, Casey and Wild Bill to tackle the mystery of Sue Ann McGee. Yes, things were changing, changing for the good! Gillie had never been ashamed of himself, but now he felt, for the first time, that he also had some people who, although maybe not his friends, were at least starting to realize that he, like all people, had a right to be himself, free of harassment and judgement. This was Gillie's finest hour.

CHAPTER 8
NEVER WAVER IN YOUR COMMITMENT

A statue can stand with a head of gold,
Seeming to emit pride brash and bold.
And its breast with polished silver may shine.
Ah, and it can have brass on its lower spine.
Iron can make the legs seem strong.
But without a core things go wrong.
Beneath, it may be built of miry clay
And reinforced with iron to prevent sway.
But Without truth it can not and will not stand.

Aaron begged Casey not to go to the Hill with him, because if anyone saw her with Aaron at Sissy Cupcheek's place, rumours would abound that she and Aaron were there to see about an illegal abortion. If her father heard about it, he would hit the ceiling with an indignant tirade of vindictiveness against Aaron and her both. Casey gave him a serious look and said, "Aaron, I have no interest in what other people think of me. I am who I am, and I am not ashamed of anything I do. As for my father, I love him dearly, but I will be 18 in two months. I am an adult, and although I intend to respect him as a parent, I do not have to respect his judgmental attitudes and tendency to look down on those who are from a lower socio-economic class than he is. If he knew I was over on the Hill mingling with blacks, he would be upset whether I was at Sissy's or not. He looks upon them as sub-human and beneath him. That is a problem he will probably never overcome. I don't have that problem, because, like you, I don't look at the colour of a person's skin. I look at the content of their character."

Aaron interjected, "but Casey……."

Before he could finish his sentence, Casey interrupted. "Don't 'but' me, Aaron Adams. We are in this together, and I am going to the Hill with you. I know you hang out over there all the time with Colon Bouton, anyway. You are always trying to pick up girls on the Hill. Have you had any luck?"

"Casey…."

Again Casey interrupted almost immediately. "It's OK, Aaron. There is nothing wrong with it for the most part." Then she smiled broadly and continued. "The problem is that you don't take the girls out in downtown Asheboro. I know that blacks aren't allowed in the theatres or restaurants, but if they were, would you take them?"

Aaron, now a bit indignant that Casey would question his integrity, replied, "I would if I could, and I freely ride around with black girls in my car, but you know it can be dangerous for them as well as for me. There are Ku Klux Klan members in this town, and like your father, my father would blow a casket if he knew I was dating a black girl. Like you, when I get 18, I will do as I please, but I see no need to antagonize him now. I will be going out-of-the-south to a university where there is not segregation, and then I will date and be seen with whomever I please. You should not be too quick to judge me. We are both products of a backward society, where people are still fighting a war that the south lost, and doing all they can to keep things the way they are, because they have been fed a steady diet of fear.

Casey, seeming contrite about her outburst, offered an apology. "I am sorry Aaron; I should not have questioned your integrity. I know what kind of person you are, and I admire you for always standing against injustice." She then smiled, almost laughing out loud as she said, "But, I am still going to the Hill with you."

Aaron shook his head and said, "of course you are!"

Winding through the affluent part of town, the two of them took in the landscape and the magnificent homes of those who lived what was referred to as the good life. Wide lawns and quiet, glassy ponds and streams, bordered by luscious, blooming rhododendrons; silent, mossy avenues, glorious with the flickering light that stole through pale green beech leaves; rose gardens with grassy paths and arbours jewel-sprinkled with shell-like petals of white, crimson, pink, and cream-like hues; magnificent homes towered over estates that were embowered with beautiful broad-leafed maple trees and fragrant, starry jasmine. This was affluence at its finest in the small town south, but it had no moral fibre beneath.

Gradually, they transitioned to the less affluent upper middle class neighbourhoods, where people, for the most part, struggled to make payments on homes they could not afford, furnished their houses with expensive extravagances and had garages filled with 2 high-priced cars that were unnecessarily luxurious. These were the people who had been brainwashed by modern media to believe that an individual's worth as a human being was defined by what he or she had. It was a world of plastic dreams with no moral core.

Gradually, Aaron's belching, smoking auto wound its way through the neighbourhood Aaron called home. They passed row after row of cookie cutter houses where the real people lived, those who were born without privilege. Those who would spend their lives struggling to keep their heads above water in a nation that was designed to serve those at the top while convincing the rest of the population that it was a nation of opportunity and that the good life was always available if people were just willing to work hard enough. The trouble was those at the top had already corned the market on the good things and there simply was no room for anyone else.

This was truly a middle class neighbourhood, where no pretentiousness was manifested. This was the place where the backbone of the country resided, living lives of inconsequence in an economic system that used them to fire the machinery that brought wealth to the few at the expense of the many. These were the people who really mattered in a world where those with prestige, privilege and wealth were exalted above all others. These were the people who should have mattered, but didn't.

Then, Casey and Aaron crossed the railroad tracks into the Hill, where the only white residents were the bootleggers who made money off serving people alcohol in a town where it was illegal. The religious element held so much sway that the residents of Asheboro were denied alcohol for fear that it would destroy the moral fibre of those who might become enslaved to the devil of drink, as if they couldn't drive 20 minutes to the next town and get it, anyway. Still, these moralists had no problem with the blacks being segregated into a slum, being denied access to the movie theatres, the restaurants and even having to use separate water fountains and bathrooms. They had no problem with a nation that was just starting to engage in an illegal and immoral war in Vietnam. They had no problem with a society that let all the benefits flow to those at the top. They had no problem with a nation that spent more money on bombs and bullets than on reaching out with the hand of compassion to people chained to the slavery of poverty. They had no problem watching people be denied healthcare because they did not have the ability to pay.

The two rolled along through the squalor of a small town slum where the black people were segregated, and from each street flashed long vistas of dilapidated homes that seemed to cry out with the misery of the people who were forced to toil in supplication to those who looked upon them as a sub-species simply because of the colour of their skin. Here and there lurched about a downtrodden and beaten individual who had simply given up on life, because of the burdens placed on them. These people had no rights in a land that promised that "all men are created equal." It was simply a worthless promise for those trapped on "the Hill."

Even the air was obscenely heavy with the intense smell of decaying hope and the repugnant scent of oppression. In one abandoned lot they passed, tottery old men and women were searching in the garbage for scraps of food, while cheerful little children clustered like flies around a festering mud hole that served as the only swimming pool for the people of colour, because they were not allowed in any of the city's pools that were reserved for whites only.

The children splashing in the mud hole were gay and carefree, unaware that, like their parents, they were destined for a life on the periphery of hope, because segregation was meant to keep them locked into submission to white America.

America was nothing more than a vast empire foundering in the hands of those who allowed man's basest instincts to subjugate fellow human beings to a life of want. Ironically, the poor whites had more in common with the blacks than they did with the white middle class and wealthy. They were both being beaten down by a system that guaranteed a permanent underclass, so that those at the top would always have a cheap supply of labour, upon whose backs they would amass fortunes. This was a system that was exalted as the greatest hope of mankind, but the hope was far too often devoured, gobbled and ravaged in the malaise of greed and self-interest.

This is not meant as an indictment of all the white individuals who lived in this little town, because most of the residents were sympathetic to the plight of the people of colour. The problem was they lived in an era and a society where speaking out for the equality of the races would get you ostracized by your friends, family and employers. A strict code of social segregation was the unwritten law of the southern United States, and anyone who dared breech it did so at their own peril. Simply by being on the Hill, Casey and Aaron were breaking a strict code that had always existed between white school students and black school students. It was an artificial barrier that simply was not to be crossed, because the result could be catastrophic according to those who ran things. The real problems, according to the guardians of moral virtue, were young black bucks who were all hell-bent on deflowering southern womanhood. This myth had been perpetuated since the end of the Civil War to keep southern men always on edge for fear that their women were coveted by black men. These manipulative manifestations of fear were often supported by religious authorities who even went so far as to say God had ordained the separation of the races when he exiled the tribe of Ham and made them black. This kind of nonsensical promotion of segregation not only trapped the blacks, but bound the poor whites who fell for the manipulations into their own form of abject slavery of the mind.

Casey, observing the poverty that abounded among these good people, turned to Aaron and said, "Why do they have to live like this? Why are they unworthy of living in the same neighbourhoods as we do?"

Aaron couldn't help but smile as he replied, "Well, some of them could maybe afford to live in my neighbourhood if they were permitted, but I don't think any of them could afford to live in your neighbourhood."

Casey shook her head and said, "You probably have a point, Aaron. However, if they could afford it, they should be allowed to live there, but they aren't."

Aaron, as he turned into his friend Colon Bouton's driveway, became contemplative in nature. "That will change some day, and it will not be the peaceful marching of Martin Luther King that does it. It will be when these people start burning down white people's homes and businesses, go into the restaurants and demand to be served, drink out of the water fountains marked whites only, and stop buying products from places that discriminate against them. You don't get your rights by going mealy mouthed to supplicate yourself and beg. You have to demand fairness; otherwise, you will not get it. Violence is the only thing that gets people's attention. You have to threaten people's safety to make them take notice. What will stop all this crap is when the white man sees it is costing him money. That is the real motivation, the only motivation in this country. Greed is at the core of all that makes this nation run. The only colour most people really care about is green. Take away the green, take money out of the white man's pocket, and then you will see some action toward fairness."

Casey, as Aaron brought the car to a halt, realized that she was amazed at his perceptiveness. "Aaron, you always have an answer that gets right at what is needed. The only problem is that it is not the answer most people want to hear, so they ignore it."

As Aaron opened his door, he looked back at Casey and said, "People ignore the truth at their own peril. Come on in and meet my buddy, Colon Bouton. We have been friends since we were 7 years old."

Casey, always mindful that men generally had to be forced into doing gentlemanly things, waited in the car for Aaron to come around and open the door for her. Actually, she didn't have to, because Aaron was going to do it anyway. He had to admit that he did it for selfish reasons, because he had learned a long time ago that being polite to girls often made them fawn over you, because most boys simply didn't act politely at the right times.

Casey looked up at him and smiled, as he gracefully opened the door for her like it was a privilege and an honour to do so. Aaron looked down longingly at her and felt a surge of those old hormones that kept wrecking havoc with him every time he got around Casey.

She was impressed with Aaron in ways that she had never been before. She had to admit it to herself; she was growing fonder of Aaron with each passing pay. In the past, she had just passed him off as a fun-loving, joking, clownish boy who lacked the seriousness she found appealing, but the real Aaron was much different.

Colon met them at the door. "Well, Aaron, I see your tastes are improving."

"Colon, this is Casey Felton. Casey meet the biggest Casanova on the Hill, Colon Bouton."

The two shook hands, and Casey said, "Well, if he is a Casanova, he needs to teach you how to improve your technique."

After a good laugh, Colon pointed at the porch swing and indicated they should have a seat as he settled into an old wooden rocking chair. "So, what brings you to the other side of the tracks?"

"Colon, don't get the wrong idea about me and Casey, but we are working on a little mystery, and we need to see Sissy Cupcheek. I know she lives over here, but I know she is a bit elusive in order to avoid the authorities."

Colon eased back in the rocker and said, "Yeah, she is always one step ahead of the police. If she isn't selling moonshine, pushing that devil weed or performing illegal abortions, she is off in New York City leading the high-life. That gal is probably the richest person on the Hill. I can take you to her. She wouldn't see you without me, though. She is really careful about meeting white people these days. The white ministers in town have been putting pressure on the sheriff to put a stop to her abortion factory. They want all those babies to be born into the good life of servitude to the rich and powerful. Funny how they want the babies to be born, but they don't want to give their parents a decent paying job so they can feed them or free medical care to keep them healthy. Let 'um be born and then to hell with 'um."

Casey offered a cogent observation as she leaned forward in the swing. "Colon, if I didn't know better, I would think those words came out of Aaron's mouth. I can tell why you two are great friends."

Colon looked at Aaron and said, "Yeah, we have been buddies since I was 7 and my dad did some work for his grandmother. She was the only white woman who ever actually had us into her house, sit us down at the table, shared lunch with us and even told Aaron he could come home with me and play. I thought it was just because she had no prejudice, but after knowing Wayne all these years, I think she was just trying to get him out of her hair."

After a good laugh at Aaron's expense, Colon got up and said, "Let's get in your chariot and take a ride to Sissy's coliseum of evil as defined by the moral guardians of virtue in this town who never do anything inappropriate themselves. If only we could all be upstanding citizens like they are."

As they rode by the Hot Spot Café, Colon, sitting in the back seat, leaned forward, tapped Casey on the shoulder and said "Ask Aaron to tell you about the first time he showed up there."

Aaron, glanced over his right shoulder and said "Colon, you aren't helping my image."

Casey, never one to be judgmental, interjected, "Nothing could give him a good image in my eyes. He is a boy isn't he?"

Aaron said, "The truth is, Colon saved my butt there one night. I just showed up, was talking with some people, trying to meet some girls, and I run across this gorgeous young lady. She is older than me, but she is really nice. You know, kind of like you Casey. She wasn't really interested, but she was too polite to tell me to take a hike."

Casey said, "Maybe she was just aware of what you were really interested in, and didn't want to encourage you."

Aaron ignored Casey's sarcasm, as Colon said when they came to the end of Leech Street, "make a left and then go onto Cedar Falls Road."

As Aaron turned left, Casey looked back at Colon and said, "I think Aaron wants to ignore the story about what happened at the Hot Spot. Maybe you better tell me."

Colon, with a smile, couldn't resist telling the story. "Well, Aaron here was trying to muscle in on a girl whose boyfriend was none other than Big Charlie Colson. Charlie shows up and takes a dim view of Mr. White Asheboro here taking a fancy to his girl. He looks at Aaron and says, 'white-boy, you in the wrong part of town, and I am going to knock you all the way back to your part of town.' Now, we both know Aaron has a reputation for never backing down from a fight."

Casey interrupted with an observation. "Yeah, he never backs down from a fight, but from what I hear, he also never wins one. If he was smart, he'd avoid antagonizing people. He would save himself a lot of physical aches and pains."

Colon had taken an instant liking to Casey, as she was not only beautiful but quick with a quip. "Yeah, you got that right. I guess it is just something about his personality that naturally antagonizes people. You noticed that, uh?"

Casey and Colon were laughing and Aaron had a scowl on his face as he said, "Who do you two have to pick on when I am not around? You are both a real riot. You should be on the Jackie Gleason Show telling jokes."

Colon replied, "We could find someone, but it wouldn't be as much fun. Anyway, back to the Hot Spot story. So Aaron is about to be the recipient of a haymaker from one Charles Colson. I happen to be pulling up about the time the fracas starts and hear the commotion, and I call over to Charlie and tell him I have something important to share with him before he sends Aaron to the Promised Land. He points his finger at Aaron and tells him not to go anywhere. Aaron is standing there all cocky, thinking Charlie must be scared of him. So Charlie comes over and I tell him that Aaron is a homo and busting him up will embarrass him more than Aaron, because he would have beaten up a gay blade who wasn't interested in his girlfriend anyway. I tell him that beating up Aaron would be like admitting he wasn't man enough for his girl to think a homo like Aaron could take her away from him. By the time Charlie found out I lied, all the furor had died down. Now he and Aaron are friends, too."

Just as Colon finished the story, he pointed to the right and said, "Turn left here on Daisy Street. She is down at the end of the street. Let me go in first and make sure everything is OK."

As they pulled into the driveway, Aaron said, "Got it man."

Casey and Aaron sat quietly. Casey was staring at him, so Aaron finally gave her a quizzical look and said, "What?"

Casey, smiling now, replied, "What? Nothing, I am just learning more about Aaron Adams every day."

Aaron smiled back and said, "lucky you."

Casey, now grinning broader, replied, "Yeah, I am lucky, lucky to know that Aaron Adams is a pretty nice guy. Anything wrong with that?"

"No, I've been trying to tell you what a nice guy I am since the second grade. You are just a slow learner. That's all."

Colon appeared at the door of the house and motioned for them to come in. The house looked a bit out of place for the Hill. It was a large two-story brick structure with two magnificent bay windows in the front and an oak entrance door that had a huge brass knocker on it. The knocker was in the shape of a nude woman, and as you walked into the foyer, two statues greeted you on either side, one a nude statue of a woman pouring water into a well, the other a nude man holding a discus with bulging sinewy muscles. From the foyer, you walked into a magnificently appointed living room that was dominated by a circular sofa in the middle that looked like it had been lifted from a Toulouse Lautrec painting. The walls of the huge room were covered in soft, bright crimson brocade that sparked with indulgent grandeur. This was an interior that not only indulged the eyes, but titillated all the senses. Aaron and Casey stood in awe, as Colon, who had been inside many times before, motioned toward a large archway to their left. Walking through the archway, they entered a library with burled walnut bookshelves lining three walls. There, sitting in a luxurious brown leather sofa, was a woman who looked like she was the dark-skinned Queen of some exotic African kingdom.

The woman stood up to greet them. She was wrapped in a layer of what appeared to be magnificent shimmering silk. At her throat was a thick collar of beige brocade embroidered with a swirling pattern of irises. Under the light blue silk was a red skirt with a quilted hem which swept to the floor and swung heavily as she moved slightly forward and on her legs was exquisite, tight fitting black silk stockings glistening with hand painted, lustrous gold flowers, swirling around her body like a train rounding a curve as it lingered to her feet. Around her waist was a swathe of orange silk brocade with a gold-thread design of chrysanthemums and maple leaves, tied in the front with an enormous knot which hung in great folds from her waist to her knees. This was the most elegant woman Aaron or Casey had ever gazed upon. And where was this magnificent looking woman of untold grandeur? Why was she on the Hill, of all places, nestled in a magnificent edifice hidden at the end of street filled with the derelicts of a society of the forgotten and enslaved? In all this squalor was magnificence as few could ever fathom in a place where dreams went to die.

The woman herself was like a majestic dignified work of art that shone with brilliance in a museum of grandeur and opulence. She was in her late 40's, and showed her age, but showed it with an eminence, fineness and glory that swept away men and women alike with awe and marvel. She had a maze of crisp black hair heaped in great wavy projections on each of her temples, a thin dark face, great thick black oblique eyebrows joined in the middle and tucking themselves away under her hair. Her long, sensuous eyelashes fluttered liked a hummingbird over a tulip greeting the morning sun. She was a woman of a tall and imposing stature, with a broad forehead, a retroussé nose and alluring dark brown eyes. Her deep red thick lips were pouty, as if ready to receive a moist kiss from a lover. She had a long, graceful neck, swelling breasts, a narrow waist accentuating generous hips and somewhat large, but still dainty feet that were necessary to balance her tall frame. She was a bright shining moon on a dark, cloudless night. Although obviously a self-confident woman in her liar of opulence, she was an egg lovingly protected in the nest, softer than fresh butter, sweeter than honey, more exquisite than paradise and eternal life. Then there was her fragrance that seemed to float on the air. It was more delightful than that of jasmine and roses and made one delight with the privilege of being in her company.

Casey leaned over to Aaron and whispered in his left ear, "down, boy, down." Because she knew he was probably valiantly fighting those raging hormones that overwhelmed young boys at the sight of such an overpowering vision of alluring beauty. Casey had to admit to a tinge of jealousy at the beauty before her.

As Colon took a seat, Sissy reached forward and shook hands with Casey and then Aaron. Casey sort of grimaced as she noticed Aaron seem to prolong the hand shake, as he was, no doubt, enjoying the feel of Sissy's sensuously soft hand. Sissy, as she pointed to a settee to her right, indicating the two should take a seat, said, "It is a pleasure to meet both of you. I have met many young people from the white high school over the years. You are a very handsome couple? What assistance may I be to you two?"

Her voice was melodious and relaxing, almost as if you knew she was a person who was there, not just for the money her services provided her, but because she genuinely cared about the welfare of those she served. The house was indeed opulent to the extreme, but one got a sense that this was a rich person with a heart, someone with wealth who never looked down at anyone, and was always ready to reach out with the hand of compassion to those in need.

Aaron's voiced quivered a little, as he was overwhelmed with Sissy's beauty and the grandeur of the place she called home. "Well, we are investigating a death from many years ago. You might remember Sue Ann McGee."

The mention of Sue Ann's name made Sissy sit up straighter and her eyes brightened. "Yes, I remember the horrible accident at the school."

Aaron, now more relaxed and comfortable, continued. "Well, we don't think it was an accident. I won't go into details about how we came to that conclusion, as it is a bit unbelievable I am afraid."

Before Aaron could continue, Sissy interrupted. "There is nothing unbelievable about a ghostly visitation. It happens all the time."

Casey and Aaron were both shocked that she would mention a ghost. Aaron could not resist pursuing her knowledge of Sue Ann McGee's ghost further. "How do you know about a ghost? We aren't even sure about it."

A slight grin crossed Sissy's lips. "Everyone has heard the stories of the ghost in the mysteriously cold corridor at the school and the many unexplainable events, including violent deaths that have occurred there. Ghostly manifestations are frowned upon by sceptics, but I am a woman who sees and hears things myself that are not within the realm of those who are less attuned to things of a more psychic nature. I have no religious beliefs whatsoever, but I do believe that death cannot always be the end of things, especially when the dead person departed the world under abnormal circumstances. Sue Ann McGee was pregnant when she died, and you are here to ask if I ever saw her in my professional capacity as a saviour of young lives that are often put asunder by hormonal urges that lead to a mistake of monumental proportions. Am I correct?"

Aaron was so mesmerized with awe by the eloquence, grace and beauty of Sissy that he simply could not reply. He stared in disbelief at a creature that overwhelmed the senses. Casey, realizing Aaron's discombobulated nature, replied, "Yes, we want to know, provided it would not violate your ethics in regards the anonymity of those you serve, if she might have paid you a visit, but more importantly, if she was with a certain young man?"

"Anonymity is for the living, not the dead. Yes, Sue Ann came to see me with a young man. The young man is still alive, so I cannot reveal his name, but I can say that he still lives here in Asheboro. Sue Ann was scheduled to terminate her pregnancy the very day after her death. She was a very fine young woman and the young man who came with her, was himself, of fine character."

Aaron, recovering from his momentary lapse into starry-eyed wonderment at the vision of incredible loveliness and grace before him, said, "OK, so you can't reveal the boy's name. I can respect that, without question. However, would it be indiscreet to describe the actions of the two?"

"Actions? We live in a country that allows abject poverty in the midst of plenty, that preaches equality and denies 10% of the population the equality that is promised and the citizens are told that they are supposed to be free to make choices about their lives, but a pack of moral hypocrites insist that the government enforce their idea of morality on the rest of us. They were two people forced by an uncaring society into coming to an untrained abortionist to help them, rather than being allowed to go to a medical facility where the procedure should have been done for free and with proper safety precautions. Yet, they did not act like the usual couple coming to take care of that type problem. There was something special about them. Most people who come to me agonize over what they are about to do, because they have been pounded and brainwashed into submission to a set of values imposed by people who, themselves, are often morally deficient. These two agonized about it, but they were deeply in love. You could see it when they gazed upon one another. The way he held Sue Ann's hand made you feel that he was more concerned about her than himself. He was agonizing, not over the baby, but over something that was beneath the surface. There was a secret the two of them were hiding. I could sense it. I wanted to probe and explore, as I felt a deep affinity for them and their predicament as I do for all those who come to me for help in dealing with an issue that is literally tearing them apart inside. Yet, I did not probe into it further. I regret that."

Aaron sensed a deep reservoir of kindness in Sissy. He thought to himself that the world of economic and moral servitude promulgated by the wealthy, the moral guardians of virtue and the government that served them was an affront to the dignity of purpose that this woman represented. She lived on the periphery of respectability while the moralistic finger pointers condemned and ridiculed as she reached out with genuine compassion for those struggling with a moral dilemma. She provided a service that many considered morally repugnant, but this woman saw it as one legitimate approach to assisting those overwhelmed by circumstance. To Aaron, those who judged and pointed the finger of condemnation were the real morally repugnant.

Casey shared her heartfelt warmth for Sissy. "Miss Cupcheek, you must not regret probing further, because it would not have prevented what happened. We think we know who the boy with her was, and it is regrettable that you found him pleasant, accommodating and devoted to Sue Ann, because we believe he could be the one of the two who might have arranged the accident."

Aaron was quick to interject, "we have no proof of that Casey. It is only supposition on our part, Miss Cupcheek. However, we think it is a well-grounded supposition, but we are still trying to piece together the facts of the whole affair. It is a crime that has been ignored for far too long, and we hope to change that."

Sissy, perceptive seer of what is in the depth of people's hearts, said, "As sure as I look at the two of you and see the deep affection you have for another, I can unequivocally tell you that the young man with her would never do anything to harm her. I have loved many men in my life and been loved in return, but I have never loved anyone, nor received the intensity of love I saw between those two."

Casey and Aaron, both shocked by Sissy sensing their affection for each other, sat in silence for a few seconds. Colon broke the silence: "They didn't realize their affection showed so much, Sissy. I knew it too, when I saw them together today. Even a blind man could see that Aaron and Casey are hot-to-trot for one another."

"Aaron, now a bit embarrassed, managed to mumble to a smiling Colon, "That is not germane to the topic, Colon. We are here to see if there is a connection between the pregnancy and the death. Sissy, you are sure they were both prepared to go through with the abortion? You saw no indication that they might back out, that they might decide to take another course of action."

"I can absolutely assure you that they had no qualms whatsoever about terminating the pregnancy. The boy assured me that they would be back the next afternoon after school with the money for the procedure. He asked if he could be by her side through the process. She smiled at him, took his hand and squeezed it lovingly."

Casey, while thinking that her affection for Aaron was now obvious to others if not even to herself, said in a contemplative tone, "We may be missing something, because all the signs indicated that there were two possible young men who might have been involved. Now, you seem to be categorically eliminating one of them. I know you are duty bound to not give us a name out of a sense of duty, ethics, discretion and respect for the boy who is now a man, maybe with a wife and children. However, could you tell us if they are both still here in Asheboro?"

Sissy, unhesitatingly replied, "Yes."

Aaron looked at Casey and they both realized that the killer could only be one of two boys, and Sissy was convinced that one of them, the one who came to her, was definitely not involved. Yet, the writing on the mirror had said: *they killed me*.

Colon, Aaron and Casey said goodbye to Sissy, and as Colon ushered them through the archway, Sissy said to the three of them: "The world is filled with people always casting about to preserve their reputation and social standing. They never face the truth of their own insignificance. Those who are earnest and willing to do what it takes to find truth, and publicly and privately avow their sympathy with the unpopular path, may be despised and persecuted for their idealism. They will bear the consequences of standing against injustice. I commend you for your tenacious pursuit of truth. Be aware and tread lightly, but never waver in your commitment."

CHAPTER 9
SHE WAS PROUD TO BE BY HIS SIDE

Scars from the past,
scars from the present,
scars from every hidden teardrop
that precipitously falls,
hiding the truth from all.
Concealing the cuts deep within the heart,
No one knows the truth of the secret love.
No one but him, and she
who sleeps in the cold ground

Gillie and Wild Bill hung on every word that flowed from the mouths of Casey and Aaron, enthralled by the tale of their meeting with Sissy Cupcheek. At school, sitting in the lunchroom, the four of them were an unlikely group: Wild Bill, the bad boy feared by all as a miscreant of mayhem; Gillie, the gay dandy who flaunted convention; Casey, the affluent miss-perfect beauty who made all the boys' hearts flutter with hormonal fury and Aaron, the class clown with a penchant for questioning authority that bordered on the obsessive. Together, the fearsome four of Asheboro youth were about to tackle more than they bargained for, as a vast array of external forces were beginning to coalesce in defence of the status-quo that had kept a dark secret for almost ten years.

Aaron was ushered into Mr. Turkian's office around 1:00 PM. The principal was a man of few words and had a sense of humour that would compare to Admiral Kimmel's when he got word that Pearl Harbour was being attacked. "Aaron, you need to go into the conference room. The Chief of Police is here to ask you a few questions."

Aaron, never one to cower before authority, very curtly replied, "I don't see any policeman without my parents being present or an attorney to represent me. I have watched enough television to know my rights. You can tell the chief to check with my parents."

Mr. Turkian, not pleased with Aaron's attitude, said, "I think young man that you better watch the way you talk."

"Mr. Turkian, I am watching the way I talk. This is supposed to be a country that guarantees people the right to counsel. I may be only 17, but I still have rights, and I am exercising them. I am going back to class. As I said, tell Chief Martin if he wants to question me about anything, he can do it at my home in the presence of my parents."

Mr. Turkian, the veins in his neck beginning to pulsate, shouted, "Listen you twerp, don't come in here and tell me how to run my school."

Aaron, very calmly, without raising his voice, almost speaking in a monotone, said, "Mr. Turkian, your job is to protect your students. My mother and father pay your salary, and they expect you to protect me when I am at school. That is your job. Allowing the Chief-of-Police to question me without an attorney or my parents is not protecting me. This is supposed to be a nation of laws. I realize that it isn't, as the law only applies to those of us with no clout while the privileged class gets a free pass.

However, I do know my rights, and nobody is going to force me to give them up, in school or out."

"You boy better watch your mouth."

"Mr. Turkian, believe me, my mouth is pretty tame compared to what you are going to hear from my father when he gets wind of what is going on. I am not being disrespectful. I am just demanding my rights as a citizen."

At the word "citizen," Chief Martin burst through the adjoining conference room door, grabbed Aaron by the arm and said, "Listen you arrogant jerk, I am here to tell you to butt out of the Sue Ann McGee affair. That case is solved and you and that gang of misfits had better watch your step. A lot of people are getting upset with your nosing around, and I am one of 'um, and believe me, you don't want to get me upset with you."

Suddenly, Mr. Turkian abruptly stood up from behind his desk and said, "Chief, I suggest you either arrest this boy or get your hands off him. You have no right to put your hands on any of my students unless they are being violent."

Looking at Mr. Turkian with shock and surprise, Chief Martin said, "You taking the side of a rebel-rousing trouble maker?"

"No, I am taking the side of a student who, unless you show me proof otherwise, apparently has done absolutely nothing illegal. I suggest you come with a warrant the next time you want to talk to Aaron."

Aaron, aghast at the sudden, abrupt, complete about-face by Mr. Turkian, stood in silent awe as the Chief let go of him, and walked out in a huff, not even bothering to reply to Mr. Turkian. Meanwhile, Mr. Turkian gave Aaron his usual authoritarian look and said, "Get back to class, Aaron."

With new found respect for Mr. Turkian, Aaron dutifully replied, "yes sir." As he got to the door, he could not resist looking back and saying, "thank you Mr. Turkian."

After school, Aaron shared what happened with his friends and assured all that he would not hold it against them if they decided to curtail their involvement in the investigation. Things were simply getting intense to the point that someone was now putting pressure on to see that the investigation was derailed. He would continue, regardless of the pressure, but he saw no need for his friends to suffer the same fate he had that day.

Determined to stick it out, they all issued stern rebukes to Aaron for even suggesting that they give up on the investigation. These four were a formable team, determined now, more than ever, to find the truth.

Casey and Aaron had avoided discussing Sissy's comments about them being enamoured with each other, but it had been preying on both their minds. On the way to see Rob Waterhouse in the afternoon, Aaron was unusually silent, but like Casey, he was reflecting upon what Sissy had said about the two of them. The closeness and affinity the two were developing for one another had never been intended by Casey. Aaron, on the other hand, had been ardently infatuated with Casey since they were in the second grade, so he was more than willing to let romance blossom.

Still, the two of them felt too inhibited to explore just what Sissy had meant. It was now a topic that had to be avoided, because each of them was struggling with the psychological aspects of the budding relationship that had been a friendship, but was now moving toward a romantic attachment.

Casey interrupted the silence with a brazen question. "We are pretty sure it was Rob Waterhouse who went to see Sissy with Sue Ann, but do you think she is right about him? Do you believe he was not involved in Sue Ann's murder? Or, could it have been him and Eric both involved?

Aaron, without hesitation, replied, "This is a bigger than two boys who were teenagers when the accident occurred. The Chief-of-Police may cater to Eric Parson because of who is father is, but make no mistake; he doesn't show up at school to warn me off the investigation just because of Eric Parson. Eric's father is also involved in some way."

Casey, now realizing that the investigation was going far beyond what she ever expected, said, "We are really ruffling the feathers of some powerful people aren't we?"

As they pulled up in front of Rob's real estate office, Aaron replied, "Don't you just love bringing down the rich and powerful? It's what I live for!"

Casey, growing more impressed with Aaron's commitment to economic and social justice in a nation that had none, found herself being drawn more and more to this boy whom she had ignored for years. He was something special, because she saw in him the inner strength that was needed to fight against a system that was always stacked against the common man. Aaron was determined to never bow before convention and accept injustice as the normal by-product of a capitalistic system. Each day, each hour, each minute she spent with Aaron only increased her respect for him as a person of deep moral conviction who was willing to always take a stand against inequity and oppression.

As they walked into Waterhouse Realty, they were greeted by a man who had worked as a projectionist for Aaron's dad when he ran the drive-in theatre. Darryl Denton was a gregarious, robust man in his 40's. Surprised at seeing Aaron, he jumped up, grabbed his hand and said, "Aaron, good to see you. How are you?"

"Good Mr. Denton, real good. I didn't know you were selling real estate."

Laughing, Mr. Denton, replied, "Truth be told, I am not selling real estate. Haven't sold anything in weeks, but I keep trying. How's your dad doing? I haven't seen him in ages."

"He is doing fine. Do you think we could see Mr. Waterhouse?"

"Rob?" Denton gestured toward the back and continued,

"Sure, go on back and knock on the door."

Aaron, realizing he had ignored Casey, quickly said, "This is my friend Casey Felton."

"Please to meet you Casey."

Casey replied, "You, too, sir."

The two of them knocked on the door and a husky, deep voice said, "Come in."

Rob Waterhouse was a good-looking man at 27, and had made a real financial powerhouse out of the business he took over from his dad when he returned from university at 22. Now, his dad was semi-retired and Rob, married with two young children, was running the number one realty firm in town. He had a lot to be proud of, but as is often the case, a great deal of his success was the result of who his father was. Aaron, as he looked around Rob's elegantly furnished office, reflected on what his own father once told him, "son, it is a lot easier to be a success when your father or mother are successes. A man who starts with a million is more likely to be a success than a man who starts with nothing. America has its own aristocracy just like Europe; only here it is based on money, rather than a title."

Rob, motioned for the two of them to have a seat as he took a seat behind his large mahogany desk. Aaron said, "Mr. Waterhouse, I am Aaron Adams and this is Casey Felton. We are conducting a personal investigation into a death at the high school back in 1953."

Rob, without hesitation, said, "I know. It is common knowledge among certain people what you are doing. I am sure you have run into some road blocks."

"We have, and we can't understand why, if it was an accident as indicated, so many people seem to be overly concerned about two high school students just asking a few questions."

Rob, a morose look slowly moving across his face, took a deep breath and exhaled with a sigh. "It causes concern because there are people who want the past buried along with Sue Ann McGee. However, I know your father Aaron, and if you are anything like him, you aren't going to let this thing go are you?"

"No sir, I am not."

Rob glanced over at Casey and said, "I am not sure some of what I am going to say is appropriate to speak about in front of a young lady."

Casey, not about to leave, spoke defiantly. "I am not easily shocked Mr. Waterhouse, and Aaron and I are in this together. Please say whatever you have to say without any thought to my sensibilities. I am a pretty down-to-earth girl who knows a bit about the realities of the world in which we live."

Rob, eased back in his chair and sighed again, almost as if he had been waiting for years to finally unburden himself of a load that was weighing heavily upon his mind. He lowered his head and wiped a tear from his eye.

Aaron, psychologically attuned to the intense need of this man to lighten a burden he had carried for so many years said, "It's OK, Mr. Waterhouse. We are not here to judge anybody. We have seen Sissy Cupcheek, and although she never betrayed the confidence of who accompanied Sue Ann to see her about an abortion, we have deduced that it was, in all likelihood, you. That it was you who had gotten her pregnant. You see, we know that you and she were meeting secretly at the Sunset movie theatre."

"The Sunset, how did you figure that out?"

"Actually, it was two of our friends who found pictures of the two of you there from old newspaper clippings, once when the MGM lion was there. So, you admit that you did meet her there."

Smiling, as if recalling it was bringing him pleasure, Rob said, "Yes, we did meet there. But you are wrong about me getting her pregnant. It wasn't me."

That statement shocked Aaron and Casey so much that they both sit up in their chairs more erect and Casey blurted out, "It wasn't you? But who was it, then?"

"That is a long story, and it is very difficult for me. You see, part of what happened to Sue Ann can be laid at my feet. I did a very unkind thing to her."

Then, Rob recounted the story of how he set-up Sue Ann for the prank that was played on her in the lunch area. "You see, I was cruel, but I realized that what I did was inappropriate, and finally I went to Sue Ann and told her how sorry I was. I didn't expect her to forgive me, but I just wanted her to know that I had remorse for what I did. Ironically, she did forgive me; although, I do not know why. The story of how we became romantically involved is something I have never shared with anyone, but if you will take a journey to 1953 and what I consider the best few months of my life, I think I might shed some light on what happened."

Aaron and Casey eased back into their chairs and started a journey back in time – a journey that would end in murder. The murder was almost 60 years ago as I write this story, so over the years what Rob shared that day has faded into the foggy, dark clouds of time, but what follows is as accurate an account as any available.

The prank that Rob assisted in playing on Sue Ann McGee in the outdoor lunch area was both a beginning and end for him. Rob agonized for weeks over what he had done, and made it a point to avoid Sue Ann, Eric and Mary Lou. However, a singular event occurred one Tuesday night that would forever change Rob's life. That event led to a relationship with Sue Ann McGee that would blossom and grow, and it also signalled an end to his association with Eric and those referred to as the blood bloods.

The weeks passed relatively uneventfully until one Friday evening, something hideous occurred that should have been reported to the police, but wasn't for a variety of reasons. It was an abomination of the foulest kind.

White Meteors and the Ghost of Sue Ann McGee

Sue Ann McGee, who worked as a waitress on the weekends at the Sidecar Café, which was right next to the Sunset Theatre, got off work at 12:00 midnight on Friday evening. Asheboro, being a town with little crime, was not a place where any girl or woman feared walking at night. However, this night someone had decided to target Sue Ann McGee for a dastardly crime of violence. As was her usual routine, she left work, said good-bye to the owner, Archie Midland, and turned down the alleyway between Hop's Bar-B-Q, which was closed, and the side of the Sunset Theatre. The narrow passageway was dark, but it was only about 30 metres long, so there was no need to be fearful, thought Sue Ann. However, as she got to the end of the alleyway, a dark figure jumped out from behind Hop's Bar-B-Q's back entrance into the alley. It was a tall, relatively thin, but muscular person dressed in black with a dark hood over the face. He grabbed Sue Ann, shoved her against the Sunset Theatre wall and said in an obviously disguised voice, "Scream and I kill you."

At that point, Sue Ann, who had never been one to react without serious thought, considered her options. She very quickly decided that the late hour would mean that no one was probably downtown, and that she was at the mercy of a man who intended her harm, but if she could remain calm; she might escape relatively unscathed with only her womanly dignity sacrificed. It was then that, as she was penned against the wall, the man leaned in very close and whispered in her ear, "you will like this bitch, I know you will." She knew what was about to occur, but decided to submit in the hopes she might escape with just the loss of her virginity rather than her life. As she closed her eyes and awaited her fate, she took a deep breath and smelled a distinctive scent that was familiar. It was a woman's perfume, a very expensive woman's perfume, but why was a man wearing a woman's perfume?

Rape is always an act of violence, and in spite of what many people say, no woman asks for it, no matter how provocatively she dresses or acts. Violence is violence, regardless of the provocation that might manifest itself in someone's mind. There is a big difference between defence and offence. "No" is as firm a word as exists in the English language. The killing of innocent women and children, the torture of prisoners, flying drones to murder designated terrorists are all acts justified by America in the war on terror, but they are absurd acts of violence, regardless of how a lawyer working for the government justifies them through legal jargon and word manipulation. That night, in the alleyway between Hop's and the Sunset Theatre, like the war criminals George W. Bush and Dick Cheney today and those who refused to prosecute them, an act of violence was sanctified in the mind of the person committing the heinous act. The victim would forever cower in fear as a result of realizing that the powerful and strong are generally immune from punishment. Sue Ann's attacker made his power clear when he whispered in his disguised husky voice, after committing his despicable act, "I am above the law, bitch. Don't forget it. You tell anyone at all about what happened here, and I will see that your mother and father are killed. Then, you will be slaughtered like a pig being butchered. Believe me, I have the power and the means to do those things and get away with it. Pull your panties up, straighten you dress and get the hell out of here." He then pointed toward the end of the alley and said, "Go bitch."

Sue Ann bowed her head and walked unsteadily out of the alley, thinking to herself that she had waited to have sex, because she wanted it to be meaningful the first time. Now, a brutal act of a thug had robbed her of that opportunity. As she leaned against the back wall of Hop's Bar-B-Q, she gathered her composure. She actually had a good idea of who the perpetrator was, and if it was the person she suspected, there would be no chance that he would suffer any dire consequences. Somehow, the blame would be turned on her, and she knew that he meant what he said about her mother and father. It was no idle threat. He was actually capable of doing what he said.

When she arrived home that night, she made the mistake so many women make when faced with how to deal with rape. This was 1953, and women not only had no control over their own bodies as a result of archaic laws promulgated by so-called moral guardians of virtue, but in many states they were classified as unable to manage their own affairs. Husbands and fathers were expected to make decisions for women. One state, Louisiana, at the time, still classified women by law as similar to what were termed morons and idiots who needed to be looked after. With this type of atmosphere, Sue Ann's reluctance to come forward and ask the Chief of Police to pursue a rapist, whom she assumed, through family connections, would be beyond reach anyway, seemed as ludicrous as expecting American businesses to share profits with their employees. It simply was not going to happen, and even if it did, Sue Ann would be made out as an enticer who lured him into the alley. Then there was that promise he had made with deep earnestness in a voice. He would kill Sue Ann's mom and dad.

Thus, Sue Ann determined that she would live quietly with what had occurred, put it out of her mind and tell no one. She resolutely refused to ever again put herself in a situation or place where such a dastardly act could occur. However, something happened about five weeks later that made it impossible to put it out of her mind. One week overdue for her monthly menstrual cycle, she began to think the unthinkable. That one act of violence had led to a pregnancy.

Another week went by, and she was now experiencing morning sickness. It was a major task to keep the secret from her parents, but she managed it. However, as she struggled with what to do, another person entered the picture who would be a knight in shining armour for her.

Rob had struggled for weeks to come to grips with his abysmal behaviour toward Sue Ann, and he finally decided that there was no way to ease his conscience other than to beg her forgiveness. When Rob apologized, Sue Ann could see the true remorse in his eyes. Seeing he was wracked with shame, she reached out and touched him on the shoulder. She smiled and said, "I am used to being ridiculed because of my poverty, so I am strong. Believe me, that incident six weeks ago is the least of my worries."

Rob, surprised at her forgiving nature, said, "Poverty and racism are the two worst kinds of discrimination. For far too long I have acceded to my friends' attitudes on race and poverty to curry favour with them, and of course, on social status as well. My father insists that I maintain certain social contacts, because he feels that success comes from those with whom you associate. He sees no advantage to being friends with those at the bottom of the social pecking order. He drags me to the country club with him, because he says you are never too young to make connections that will foster your rise to prominence later. I am afraid he has my entire life mapped out for me. I am destined to work in his firm and become even more successful than he is. It's almost as if he thinks my success is his success. I am afraid I disappoint him in many ways, because I am not aggressive enough in pursuit of social acceptance by the elite of this town."

Sue Ann, with sincere earnestness, said, "That is a very eloquent way of putting it Rob. It is admirable that you would be concerned about my feelings and those of others who have been targeted by a group of people who think they are somehow better than others because who their parents are. That is the way of a world where everything is based upon what you have, rather than who you really are as a person, deep inside. Character should matter more than money. I know you are from a wealthy family, but I have never had the feeling that you thought yourself better than those less fortune than you. I could never understand why such a nice person hung out with such a pack of arrogant, self-absorbed jerks. Now I understand, because at our age, we are often pawns in the hands of parents who want to shape and mould us into what they want, rather than allowing us to seek our own destiny. My poverty stricken parents, fortunately, are not that way, but I do see it often among my friends' parents. Many parents are over compensating for their own failures in life by putting undue pressure on the children to do that which they were incapable of doing themselves."

Rob, sincerely impressed by Sue Ann's compassion and intelligence, blurted out something that surprised them both, "Want to go to the movies tonight?"

Sue Ann, flattered that Rob would ask, said, "I would love to go with you, but I don't think it is good for you to be seen with me right now. After all, the blue bloods can make things miserable for you, and with only a few months of school left, there is no need antagonize them. Also, your father would be distressed that you were seeing someone out of your social class. I just wouldn't fit into what he has planned for you. I have heard about your dream to attend Princeton. You don't want to throw away your future on a foolish whim. Anyway, believe me; I am facing some serious problems right now that probably wouldn't make me very good company."

Rob, deep within, wanted to throw caution to the wind, but he knew that his future was dependent on a father who would whimsically forbid to finance his education if he dared defy him, and letting his father know that he was seeing someone of Sue Ann's social status would be a sure way of cutting off his hope of attending Princeton, which had been a dream of his since he was 12 years old. He hung his head in shame as he said, "Yes, I do have a lot to lose, but maybe we could go to the Sunset Theatre separately, and then meet up in the balcony. I know it is shameful of me to suggest it, but I want to spend time with you Sue Ann. Hey, maybe I could help you with those problems you say are bothering you. I am pretty good listener. What do you say? Come on; give a guy a chance to really make-up with you. Let me spend 75 cents to take you to a movie. I'll even buy you some popcorn."

Sue Ann, who had always been attracted to Rob, simply could not resist. Forgetting her troubles for a second, she enthusiastically replied, "O.K., you've got a date. But how are you going to pay my way when we are going in separately?"

Rob reached into his pocket and took out three quarters. Handing them to her, he said, "My treat, and I'll have two boxes of popcorn when we meet up in the balcony. *What Ever Happened to Baby Jane* is playing. I love Bette Davis. She can be so evil."

Sue Ann smiled, nodded her head and said, "Being evil is easy for some people. Unfortunately, not all people are acting like Bette Davis does. Some people are genuinely evil."

Rob did not reply, but on the way home he thought over what Sue Ann had said. He wondered if what she said was a bit of a dig aimed at him. He would find out it was something much different, something deeply sinister and foreboding.

That was the first of many times they slipped into the Sunset Theatre, often seeing the same movie two, three or even four times. Over the next week, they were there constantly. Yet, Rob had never attempted to even hold her hand, but one Thursday night as they sat watching the epic *Lawrence of Arabia*; Rob reached over in the darkness, took her hand and gently held it. Sue Ann, who had been struggling with depression over her predicament, felt Rob's warmth and tilted her head so that it rested on his shoulder.

Rob nuzzled a bit closer, and Sue Ann whispered, "I need to talk to somebody about a predicament I am in Rob. You think we could go somewhere quiet, just the two of us? I will leave and walk over to the Anchor Building. We could sit in your car behind the bus station and talk."

Without hesitation, Rob replied, "Sure, let's go. We'll come back and watch the movie another time."

Rob wanted to just walk out with her, but Sue Ann insisted they not do it. To her, it was now a matter of protecting Rob from the wrath of a father who simply could not see the real worth of his son was not in his social contacts, but in the depth of his empathy for those of meagre means and pitiful circumstances.

As they sat in Rob's car behind the bus station, Sue Ann broke down in tears and shared with him exactly what happened that night in the alley. Rob, overwhelmed with anger, said, "I'll kill him. I'll kill him."

Sue Ann gently offered a more sober approach. "That is not the answer Rob. Anyway, I have no specific proof who it was, only an inclination. There was something unusual about the man. I can't put my finger on it, but there simply was something strange about the guy. But, you haven't heard the worst of it, yet. I am pregnant!"

Rob bowed his head and sighed. "Pregnant! What luck! Sue Ann, why didn't you go to the police?"

"I have my reasons, Rob."

J. Wayne Frye

"Sue Ann, you are allowing a rapist to be on the loose."

Sue Ann took a deep breath. "Yes, but he said that he would kill me, my mother and father if I went to the police, and that he had the power to do it. I think I know who it is, but it does me no good, because of where I come from."

Rob, his intense rage slowly fading into concern and compassion, said, "In a few more months you are going to have his baby."

Sue Ann, with deep and contemplative sorrow, almost mournfully interjected, "I don't want to have the baby Rob, but we live in a country that forces a young girl to follow the dictates of hypocritical finger pointers who have no real compassion outside their own narrow definitions of morality."

Rob, aware of the dilemma she was facing, said, "I will do all I can for you Sue Ann. I would even marry you if necessary to save your honour."

Sue Ann was overwhelmed with deep affection for Rob. His concern made her realize the real depth of his feelings for her. How incredibly ironic she thought that it took tragic circumstances for the two of them to find one another.

Rob insisted on taking her home. He turned left onto Sunset Street, rode past the theatre again and made a right onto Park Street. As he was waiting to turn left at the light on Park and Fayetteville Street, Sue Ann slipped over a little closer to him and leaned her head onto his right shoulder. Rob turned left and did not notice the Cadillac waiting at the stop light as they turned. However, in that car was a man seething with rage at what he saw. Don Waterhouse knew Sue Ann McGee, but worse, he knew her parents, and realized that his son Rob was taking her to Peachtree Street, which in 1954 was one of the poorest sections of town, and he knew right where he was headed – to an old converted barn behind a duplex where Sue Ann's parents lived in abject poverty. His anger was building to a fever pitch as he made a turn into Voncannon's Texaco Service Station, swept between the gas pumps and spun back onto Fayetteville Street, picking up his son's tail lights just as Rob turned onto Peachtree Street. The light was red, so he had to wait, his anger continuing to build to a fever pitch. Rob, at Sue Ann's urging, let her off at the dirt driveway to the barn which sat about 25 metres behind the duplex. She gave him a light kiss on the cheek and said, "See you tomorrow."

Rob, glancing at his rear view mirror, noticed headlights coming up Peachtree, as he replied, "You can depend on it." He waited patiently as Sue Ann made her way up the driveway and around the back of the duplex. Just as he was about to pull-off, his dad's Cadillac pulled up beside him and Rob's heart starting pounding furiously. His dad pointed forward with his index finger, indicating Rob was to follow him home.

At home, the fury of his father continued for almost an hour, until Rob agreed that he would abstain from seeing Sue Ann again. He hated lying to his father, but felt it was the best approach to avoiding any more verbal abuse.

J. Wayne Frye

A couple of weeks later, in the cafeteria, Mary Lou and Eric looked over disdainfully at Rob and Sue Ann as they shared lunch in what had become the norm at school for the two of them. In fact, although Rob and Sue Ann had kept themselves free from discovery by meeting clandestinely in the balcony of the theatre, word had spread among the students that there was a suspected romantic relationship between them. Fearful of Rob's father's reaction, Sue Ann and Rob continued to avoid being seen in public places outside of school. However, they had taken to driving to nearby Greensboro, which was 30 minutes away, where they could freely experience the joys of sharing a romantic relationship.

Eric and Mary Lou could not help but ask themselves what Rob was doing with someone whom the blue bloods had designated as a target of their wrath and indignation. Meanwhile, Rob whispered to Sue Ann, "I will not put pressure on you to share that which you do not want to share, but if you think you recognized who it was, I would like to know.

Sue Ann, flattered that Rob was so concerned about her, replied, "I do not want to get you in trouble, Rob. I am afraid of what you might do. Your concern for me is commendable, but I am not 100% sure. All I know is that there was an unusual scent to him. I think he was wearing a woman's perfume, or had been with a woman who was wearing a very expensive perfume and some of it got on him. Please don't ask me to accuse someone who might well be innocent. Suspicion does not mean guilt. I simply cannot, at this time, categorically accuse someone. Rather, I must decide what to do about the pregnancy."

Rob, familiar with Sissy Cupcheek as a dependable source for terminating pregnancy, said, "I know someone on the Hill, who can take care of the problem, if that is what you desire."

"Rob, I have no religion to interfere with my decision, so I am ready to do what I must in order to preserve my dignity and my future. I willing to get an abortion.. First, I must procure the amount of money needed. This is a country where avenues to relieve distress like this are closed to those without money."

Rob replied earnestly, "I will give you the money."

"I know you will, but I must do this myself. It is not your fault I am in this predicament, and I would not feel right taking the money from you."

Rob, more serious than Sue Ann had ever seen him, replied, "Then, I will lend you the money. Pay me back when you can."

"You are a good person, Rob. I shall accept your offer of money and help. I will pay you a little bit every two weeks out of my meagre earnings at the restaurant."

"Done, and you still have a few weeks, so just let me know when you want to do this. I am here to help anyway I can. Hey, the MGM lion is going to be at the Sunset tonight. Let me get your mind off this. I'll treat you to a movie. We can even go out in plain sight. I am tired of hiding in the shadows and always going to Greensboro to avoid people we know."

Sue Ann, ever cognizant of the tenuous situation Rob was in because of his father, replied in a stern manner. "I will go, but only if we do it the old way. A few weeks ago, we went and I you touched my hand as we were going into the lobby. That was not a good idea. I felt preying eyes all around us. I am afraid that we are not fooling that many people. We'll see the lions and then we go in separately, like always. Maybe the day will come when we can be more open and not worry about your dad, but I am not going to let you jeopardize your future, especially after he saw you taking me home that night. I know you told him it was just a courtesy lift, but he is no fool. Everyone is beginning to see that we have an interest in one another. Even my friends are hinting that I am romantically involved with you."

"OK Sue Ann. You win. We'll do it your way.'

Smiling broadly, Sue Ann replied. "Of course we will!"

That was the night that Eric showed up at the theatre and cast a weary eye on Sue Ann and Rob that was caught on camera. Within a few days, Sue Ann would be dead."

Thus ended Eric's recounting of his relationship with Sue Ann McGee.

Casey, ever the romantic could not resist saying, "you were really in love with her weren't you Mr. Waterhouse?"

Smiling, as if recalling a pleasant time of his life, Rob replied. "Still am."

Those words penetrated Aaron and Casey's hearts, because they knew that Rob was married to Alicia Anderson and had two young children. Still, he could not put his love of Sue Ann out of his mind.

Realizing what he had said, Rob very quickly countered by saying, "Of course, I love my wife and children, but there are some things you just can't get over. I hope you will keep what I just said in confidence."

Aaron was quick to reply. "Of course we will. Everything we discuss here today is between us and no one else. I know you married Alicia Anderson, who apparently had a big fight with Mary Lou Hinton over Eric. Has you wife ever mentioned anything that might be of help to us?"

"Not really, basically our marriage was arranged between our families. Neither one of us have the courage to stand-up to our parents, even today. It is a sad state of affairs for two adults to have no backbone when it comes to parents, but it is just the way it is. We are both just pawns to our parents on the chessboard of life. We never really mention her brief fling with Eric back in high school. Eric was a heartthrob, and very few girls would not succumb to his charms. We avoid Eric and his wife at any social functions. That old animosity is still there between all of us."

Casey looked at Aaron, almost as if saying, "I pity poor Rob." Aaron acknowledged her with a nod as he continued with his questioning. "You say that Sue Ann felt her rapist was either wearing a woman's perfume or had recently been with a woman who wore heavy perfume?"

"Yes, she did say that, and I know it preyed upon her mind often. She just steadfastly refused to share her suspicions with me for fear that I might do something rash. She was probably wise in doing so, because I was so much in love with her that the thought of anyone doing that to her filled me with rage."

Aaron, nodding in agreement, said, "Understandable." Then he looked over at Casey and continued, "I would feel the exact same way."

There was a sincere simpatico developing between Aaron and Rob, and it made Aaron feel that he could ask him almost anything. In fact, his next several questions were going to be a bit risqué, and he hated to have to ask them in front of Casey, but knew that she would be offended if he suggested she leave. "I realize this is a delicate question, and if you do not want to answer, I understand. I am asking it, because it goes to the heart of what I am beginning to suspect. Were Mary Lou Hinton and Eric still seeing each other when Sue Ann was raped?"

"They were. After the big fight between Mary Lou and Alicia , Eric and Mary Lou, as they always did, drifted back together, because frankly they were perfect for each other. Both of them were jerks."

Now, Aaron was ready for the big question. "And was Mary Lou just as unfaithful as Eric?"

A hint of contempt flashed in Rob's eyes. "She was. How did you know?"

Casey couldn't help but interject, "We've seen Mary Lou. She does not strike me as they type of woman who could ever be completely faithful to one man."

"She enjoyed teasing boys, and from what I heard, even men. She was not particular about the age of those whom she tantalized."

Aaron was on a roll and ideas were jumping about in his head like the proverbial Mexican jumping bean. "Now the big question Rob. Did Mary Lou always wear expensive heavy smelling perfume?"

Suddenly, Rob's mind flashed back to what Sue Ann had told him years ago in regards to the rapist wearing what smelled like expensive women's perfume. Overflowing with emotion, his voice quivering, he replied, "yes, yes, she always had tons of that stuff on. You could smell her coming down the hall from 20 feet away. Why didn't I realize it when Sue Ann mentioned it? Yes, it had to be Eric who raped her. He had been with Mary Lou before and still had the smell of her perfume on him."

Aaron, ever the weary investigator, said, "Maybe yes, maybe no. You just said that Mary Lou was rather free with her charms and was apparently unfaithful to Eric. Consequently, although I agree the finger of suspicion points decidedly toward Eric, it is not conclusive, and it could have even been a man who was indeed wearing women's perfume or a man had been with a woman who did wear heavy perfume, maybe not Mary Lou. I never conclude anything until the facts seem to add up in a categorical configuration that points to a definitive result. I have had my suspicions about a lot of things since we visited Mary Lou, but don't overreact right now. Give us a few days and we are going to find out something big, really big."

Rob, now thoroughly convinced that there was something deeply sinister about the whole affair, could not help but blurt out, "her death absolutely was no accident then."

Aaron very calmly, but in a determined manner replied, "She was murdered."

"And you suspected me?"

Casey and Aaron looked at one another and Casey replied, "We did, but I think I speak for myself and Aaron when I say that now we don't."

Aaron, looking directly at Rob, said, "Affirmative."

"You have any idea who it was?"

Aaron, feeling somewhat smug about how he was beginning to put the pieces of the puzzle together, replied, "I do. I really do, but I am not ready to reveal it just yet. I do have one other question for you, Mr. Waterhouse."

"Sure, go ahead."

"You were the mysterious cloaked figure at Sue Ann's funeral, first at the nearby grove of trees and then over her graveside. Am I right?"

A faint smile crossed Rob's lips. "I am the one."

Aaron looked at Casey, then back at Rob. "We are going to Mr. and Mrs. McGee's to ask a few more questions. Would you like to go along and tell them about your romance with Sue Ann? I think they would like to hear it. I believe they would be comforted to know she had such a good friend in her final days."

Casey felt a surge of respect and admiration for Aaron. She saw him as an extraordinary young man capable of deep compassion. She was proud to be by his side.

.

CHAPTER 10
LET'S ROCK AND ROLL

When truth comes, the landscape listens.
Shadows hold their breath in anticipation.
When truth lights the night with brightness,
Injustice is rectified and sanctity prevails.

That night at Sue Ann's parents' home, tears of relief were cried by all present. There was a cathartic release of tension that had built up over the years as Rob Waterhouse, Mary McGee and Frank McGee warmly embraced. Finally, Rob was prepared to let the world know that he had loved Sue Ann. He would go home to his wife and share with her the pain he had carried so long. He would beg her to understand that which he had been unable to share. That which he felt had kept him from loving her the way he should have. Maybe they could find the peace they needed to carry on and live a good life. And he was prepared to finally confront his father with the truth also. To let him know that Rob should be allowed to live his life as he saw fit, not as an extension of what his father desired.

Aaron and Casey had picked up Gillie and Wild Bill, and they all shared with Sue Ann's parents what they had discovered. The evening brought some peace to Sue Ann's parents after all those years. Yet, there was one lingering question that needed to be asked. It was Frank McGee who looked at Aaron and said, "Who Aaron, who killed my lovely daughter? Who?"

"That sir is something I am not sure of yet."

Frank, sitting beside Rob, got up, walked to the window and looked out into the darkness. "You think you know don't you?"

Aaron very carefully replied, "I do, but I must be sure. Mr. McGee, it was not just one person. It was more. One person may have tampered with the rope, but there were others involved. Be patient another day or two, and I think we can arrive at the truth. It will rock this town to its core, but there are good people here, and they will demand justice for Sue Ann."

That night as Gillie, Wild Bill, Casey and Aaron drove away from the McGee's, the four of them were very pensive as each person was overwhelmed by what had occurred. It was Gillie who broke the silence. "Aaron, you do not have to share what you know, because I realize that you are worried about accusing the wrong people, but can you please tell me one thing?"

Aaron, anticipating his question, said, "No, I actually don't think Eric raped Sue Ann, but I think he knows who did. Tomorrow, Casey and I are going to see Eric. Then we are going to visit Mary Lou again." Casey glanced at Aaron, totally unaware of what he had in mind, but she was confident in his ability to get the truth.

Aaron continued. "Mary Lou has been keeping a secret, too. Something Rob said about her made me realize it. You see, Mary Lou said something that made me think that there was another more sinister element involved. Gillie and Bill, I want you two to study that picture with Rob, Sue Ann and Eric in it."

J. Wayne Frye

Casey, intrigued, said, "And what are they looking for?"

Aaron replied, "They are looking for an older man, standing beside Eric. Take heed you two. Study the photo closely and identify who the older man is. I think I know, but I want to be sure."

Aaron was going to drop the two boys off at their respective homes, but when he arrived at Gillie's, Wild Bill hopped out of the car and said, "I'm spending the night at Gillie's."

Aaron and Casey quizzically looked at one another. They watched the two boys cheerfully going up to Gillie's front porch. As Aaron drove off, Casey said, "You don't think, do you? Nah, it couldn't be. It couldn't, not Wild Bill? Gillie yes, but Wild Bill, no way."

The two of them said nothing more about it. Rather, they concentrated on what they were going to do the next day. When Aaron arrived at Casey's home, her dad was actually waiting on the front porch with his arms crossed and a stern look of disapproval on his face.

Casey ignored her dad, smiled at Aaron and said, "I was real proud of you today, Aaron."

She leaned over, gave him a kiss on the cheek and scurried up the porch steeps, greeted her dad with smile and said, "Great night, dad. Better get used to Aaron dropping me off, and soon I will be inviting him in. You see, I am developing a real affection for him. So, you better get used to it. Good night!"

She had said it loud enough for Aaron to hear, but the car windows were rolled up, and he was frantically backing out of the driveway for fear that Casey's father might actually walk up to the car and tell him to stay away from his daughter; consequently, he had missed a performance that was meant as much for him as for Casey's father.

The following afternoon, Casey and Aaron showed up at Parson manufacturing to meet with Eric Parson. The nearly 10 years since high school had not been overly kind to him. He had lost most of his hair and he had put on a mass amount of weight. He greeted them less than cordially, pointed to a thick, luxurious leather sofa and never even bothered to shake hands. Sitting behind a huge, kidney shaped desk with leather inlays around the edges and a cigar in his mouth, the only thing that was missing from the image one usually has of a titan of industry was a little more age. He was very abrupt. "Time is money. State your business, please."

Aaron, as usual, not intimidated by power and wealth, leaned forward a bit and said, "You know why we are here."

Eric, surprised, as was Casey, by Aaron's abrupt manner, replied, "So I do. Word has gotten out about your little amateur investigation. You two are going to get yourself into some big trouble."

Aaron was going to enjoy this. "I live for trouble Eric." He didn't call him Mr. Parson, because he wanted to make sure that Eric knew he was not intimidated by him.

Eric said, "Kid, I know you and I know that womanizing, drunkard father of yours, too. Don't come in here all high and mighty."

Aaron was just getting warmed up. "My father drinks too much, and he does like the ladies. However, we aren't here to discuss him or his bad habits. I do not know about your drinking habits, but I do know that you have always thought of yourself as a ladies man, today and in high school. Want to talk about how you were attracted to someone you didn't want anyone to know you were interested in?"

"What are you hinting at?"

Aaron, smiling now, continued, "I am talking about how your hormones went into overdrive every time you looked at Sue Ann McGee."

Eric leaned forward with a look of disgust. "You don't know what you are talking about."

Aaron was enjoying the verbal sparing. "That's not what Mary Lou says."

"Mary Lou? You have been talking to her?"

Aaron was nonchalant in his reply. "We talk to a lot of people, Eric. In fact, you would be surprised at some of the things we have found out. Are you a little nervous?"

"I have nothing to be nervous about. You are a couple of high school kids on a wild goose chase."

Casey, who had sat quietly, realized that Aaron was playing his old game of bad guy – good guy. She very demurely said, "Please excuse Aaron's rudeness, Mr. Parson. He is sometimes overzealous. We just want to ask a few simple questions that might help in our investigation. No one is here to accuse you of anything. We were just wondering if you might be able to shed some light on who the father of her child might have been."

Aaron leaned back and let Casey take the lead. He now had Eric where he wanted him. Casey, realizing Eric's interest in women, crossed her legs to get his attention. It worked. Eric's eyes lit up and he said, "I am not certain who the father was. I know she and Rob Waterhouse were dating clandestinely for awhile. They thought it was a secret, but it wasn't."

Then Casey hit him with question that generated a shock. "You followed Rob and Sue Ann to the Sunset movie theatre on occasion?"

"How did you know that?"

"We may be high school kids, but we do have our methods."

Eric, still shocked that they knew, replied, "I followed them there a couple of times. They would slip to the back of the balcony."

Aaron couldn't resist. "And you were envious of Rob weren't you?"

Without hesitation, Eric replied. "Yes, maybe I was. Sue Ann was a good looking girl, a beautiful girl in fact. Rob had been my closest friend for many years, and he dumped me because of a silly little prank I played on Sue Ann."

Aaron looked at Casey, as if to signal her that she should proceed with the questioning, because Eric was now antagonistic toward him. She did. "So, Mr. Parson, did you know that Sue Ann was raped?"

Suddenly, Eric sat up straighter and he blinked his eyes, as if surprised. "Raped?" He then took a deep breath. "Raped?"

Casey, realizing that he was either genuinely shocked or putting on a good act, said, "Yes, she was raped. In fact, the rape resulted in the pregnancy."

Eric seemed to drift off into a trance. He was mulling over what had been shared by Casey. Meanwhile, Aaron, ever observant, took in the complete reaction and said, "Are you shocked that she was raped, or are you shocked that we knew she was raped?"

Eric seemed unable to answer. He just stared at Aaron. Aaron got up, walked to the desk and said, "My guess is that you are not surprised about the rape, but you are shocked we knew, because you know who the rapist was, don't you?"

Eric's face was getting red, and his breathing became shallower. "Out, both of you, out!"

Aaron turned his back to Eric, motioned for Casey to get up and they walked toward the door. He abruptly stopped and turned back to Eric with some parting words. "Get all your ducks in a row, Eric. You are going to have to get your lies straight. You high and mighty, privileged, arrogant, aristocratic acting wealthy barons think you are above the law, but sometimes, yeah sometimes, you come up against someone like me who loves to bring you down from your pedestals. Even the mighty sometimes can fall. Get ready to rock and roll, buddy!"

Aaron slammed the door so hard that he thought the glass might break. Casey took his arm, leaned against his shoulder and whispered, "who you bringing down next, tiger?"

Aaron smiled and said, "Casey, my girl, wouldn't you like to know."

On the way out of Eric's office, they passed through a secretarial pool. One of the girls jumped up, and as she was headed toward the water cooler, she bumped into Aaron and slipped a small piece of paper into his left hand. He waited until they got to the parking lot to look at it. He opened his hand and in small letters was a note stating, *you need to see me. I get off work at 4:30. Meet me at the Blue Mist Café.*

Casey said, "you know who that was, Aaron?"

"No."

"That was Ellen Stutts."

Aaron pulled up to the Blue Mist and as was typical of those days, a waitress on roller skates came out to the car to take the order. Aaron asked Casey if she wanted anything and she said, "Cherry Coke would be nice."

Aaron said, "One Cherry Coke and one Vanilla Coke."

As they sat there contemplating why Ellen Stutts wanted them to meet with her, Aaron observed a blue Chevrolet parked by the side of the road across the street from the Blue Mist. He had noticed it follow them out of the Parson Manufacturing parking lot. The engine was running and the person behind the wheel was an older man, but he was too far away for Aaron to really get a good look at him.

Aaron kept glancing up at his rear view mirror. The waitress brought the cokes in frosted glasses and Aaron raised his window just a bit, so the waitress could put the tray down on the side of the car. He paid, and as the girl was making change, Casey reached up and adjusted the rear view mirror to where she could see across the street. As the waitress was leaving, she said, "He followed us from the Parson Plant didn't he?"

"Yes, my guess is that Eric made a quick call to one of his flunkies and told him to follow us and see where we went. This could get Ellen Stutts in trouble, if she is seen with us."

Casey took a sip of her Cherry Coke, handed it back to Aaron and said, "relax, it's 4:25. I can have this guy out of here in five minutes."

Parked three cars down was an Asheboro police car with none other than old cigar chomping Frankie Pernell sipping on a root beer. Like clockwork, he drove from the police station and showed up at the Blue Mist around 4:15 to 4:20 for his daily root beer.

Casey strolled up to his car and said, "Hello Officer Pernell."

"Howdy there Casey Felton. How you doing?"

"Pretty good," said a perky acting Casey. "But, you see that blue Chevrolet over there across the street parked in that no parking zone?"

Frankie was what the local kids called their very own Barney Fife, who was the bumbling sheriff's deputy on the hit Andy Griffith Show that was so popular on television. He fumbled with his root beer and started to look back at the Chevrolet but Casey whispered, "don't let him see you looking Officer Pernell. You see, my friend and I noticed that when we went by the elementary school he was parked there watching the kids walk home. Then, he pulled in over there like he is waiting for some of them to walk up this way. Seems like a very suspicious character."

Frankie signalled the waitress as he placed his root beer on the tray. "Take it away miss. I'm on the job."

As the waitress took away the tray, Frankie got out and Casey said, "We all feel so safe Officer Pernell when you are on the job.

Pernell puffed out his chest and strode toward the Chevrolet, his shoulders thrown back and a cocky look on his face. Casey returned to the car and told Aaron, "Casey Felton, little Miss Manipulator."

Aaron smiled and said, "I won't ask what you told him, but take a look."

Casey glanced across the street and Asheboro's Barney Fife had the man out of the car, bent over the hood and was frisking him just as Ellen Stutts pulled into the Blue Mist. Aaron pointed with his index finger toward the back of the building, signalling that was where he wanted to talk. She pulled around to the back and Aaron followed.

Aaron and Casey got out of the car, went over to Ellen and she motioned with her head for the two of them to get in. Aaron got in the front and Casey got in the back. Ellen looking somewhat excited, said, "I have heard that you two are investigating Sue Ann McGee's death. Are you aware of what happened to me one night in that locker room?"

Casey, resting her hands on the back of the front seat, said, "We know about all the things that happened in that area. There were two deaths, two boys were unhinged mentally and one of those two committed suicide. They tried to rape you and apparently one of the boys had a change of heart and took out his wrath on the others."

Shaking her head and almost laughing, Ellen said, "No, it was no change of heart. All four tried to rape me. What stopped it was Sue Ellen McGee."

Aaron, ever the sceptic, said, "So, a year after her death, Sue Ellen comes to your rescue?"

"I don't expect you to believe me. I knew then that no one would. That is why I never told anyone that I saw Sue Ellen McGee in the form of a vapour or mist. She is the one who saved me. I saw the terror on those boys' faces, but I never had any fear, just amazement, because I knew whatever it was would not do me any harm."

Casey said, "I believe you, and so does Mr. Not-So-Sure over there. The truth is that we didn't see her specifically, but she did communicate with us in her own way. We are convinced her death was no accident. It was murder."

"That is why I am here. I heard about the investigation you two are conducting. You see, something very strange happened a few days ago. As you know, I am in the secretarial pool. Well, I was taking some papers in for Eric Parson to sign. As is customary, I knocked on the door. He said, 'just a minute.' I stood there for a good two or three minutes, just waiting for his highness to deem me worthy of being in his presence. I hear some papers being shuffled and realize he is talking on the phone. He was whispering, but I could still hear some of what he was saying."

Aaron, with intense curiosity, said, "It had to do with Sue Ann McGee, right?"

Ellen replied, "You bet it did and that is not all. I found out even more."

White Meteors and the Ghost of Sue Ann McGee

Casey encouraged her to continue. Very deliberately, Ellen said, "You see, I leaned in really close to the glass part of the door and heard him say, 'I am telling you that we are all doomed for the acts of a stupid man who couldn't keep his pants zipped around that piece of white trash. We will all go down for his stupidity. Our exalted positions in this community will not keep us from paying the piper on this one.' I just stood there mystified, because I knew he was talking about Sue Ann McGee."

"And how did the conversation conclude," asked Aaron.

"He simply said that they would take the necessary actions. But what really concerns me is you two. You see, when I eventually was told to come in, I stood there in front of his desk, handed him the papers and I noticed something written on the notepad on his desk. The words were upside down, but it was your names – *Aaron Adams and Casey Felton*. So, I think you should know that you may not be safe. The Parson's are not the kind of people you want to have as enemies. They are ruthless in business and in everything else they do. Eric is bad, but his dad is even worse. If he is involved, watch out."

Aaron said, "Thank you for your concern Ellen, I know you are risking your job by doing this. We appreciate your concern for us, and we will be very cautious. I assure you."

Ellen smiled and said, "Sometimes I would like to get fired. You have no idea how they treat their employees. They have gotten rich off the backs of those they have contempt for."

Aaron replied, "That is the way of the world, unfortunately. There is nothing but contempt from those at the top for the very people who oil the machinery of capitalism that puts money into the pockets of those who couldn't last an hour on the factory floor actually doing some real work."

Ellen gave Casey a quizzical look. Casey said, "Yes, I know, he can get a bit melodramatic when it comes to the working class. That is the type of rhetoric he spouts constantly. He thinks he is a revolutionary who will one day lead a rebellion against the privileged class and institute a utopian workers' paradise."

Ellen, smiling, looked at Aaron and said, "Count me in!"

They parted and as Ellen drove off, Aaron said to Casey while they sat in the car, "Life can only be understood backwards; but it must be lived forwards. We are onto not just a murder, but a conspiracy to cover it up. I am scared for you Casey. I think it best that you maybe let me pursue this on my own now. Even Gillie and Wild Bill might be at risk."

"Well, Mr. Aaron Adams, no way. I appreciate your concern. It is what I would expect from a person as gallant as you are. However, I am just as determined as you are to see this through to the end. Don't even think that I am going to be excluded at this point. What's next on the agenda?"

Aaron shrugged his shoulders and said, "Mary Lou!"

As they pulled out onto the highway, they saw the blue Chevrolet and Officer Frankie "Barney Fife" Pernell was walking away from the car with his chest puffed out and a big grin on his face, apparently content that he had issued a stern warning to a miscreant who dared entertain any thoughts of wrong-doing on his beat.

Before going to Greensboro to see Mary Lou, the two decided to stop at Hop's for a bite to eat. That stop would actually wind up preventing them from ever seeing Mary Lou again.

Casey knew that Aaron was on to something big in regards to Mary Lou, but she had learned that he had a flair for the dramatic, so she decided to bide her time and let him tell her about it when he was ready. He just loved playing detective, and she actually enjoyed watching him. The guy she had avoided a romantic entanglement with for so long had finally titillated her interest after all those years.

The drive to Greensboro was one of great anticipation for Aaron and Casey, but as they approached the gate that was used to protect the rich from the ordinary people, there was a line of cars waiting to get in. Looking at the short stone fence that surrounded the community, Aaron could not help but almost laugh at the false security that was promised by a gate. Weren't the rich, arrogant, self-absorbed, privileged classes who hid behind their gates aware that any reasonably nimble person could just hop over the waist-high stone wall? Maybe they thought the mere presence of a gate was deterrent enough to keep the riff-raff from breeching the sanctity of their monuments to excess and greed.

Many of the drivers and passengers were lingering outside their automobiles, engaged in frantic conversation with looks of shock on their faces. Casey and Aaron got out, and Aaron asked a man in front of him what was going on. The man, visibly upset, replied, "Cops shut the whole place down – nobody in or out. Been a double murder and suicide. Billy Hindle's wife has been killed, apparently by a lover who also shot the butler and then committed suicide. Always knew that gold-digger was no good."

Aaron ushered Casey back to the car. They got in, turned around and headed back for Asheboro. Casey was visibly upset, as things seemed to be spiralling out of control. She begged Aaron to tell her what he was going to ask Mary Lou.

Aaron sighed deeply, and spoke very softly, "She said something when we were there that took awhile for me to figure out, because I was distracted by her alluring nature. First, I want to check with Gillie and Wild Bill about that photo. If they found what I think they did, the most prominent family in Asheboro is about to be brought down from their high and mighty perch of superiority."

"But Aaron is Mary Lou's death connected to our investigation?"

"I am afraid it is. She knew something that Sue Ann's killers didn't want to get out. The odd thing is that Mary Lou didn't even know what made her a threat to them, because she was not aware that Sue Ann had been raped in that dark alley between Hop's and the Sunset Theatre. I am afraid we brought the past back into her life, and she paid for something she did years ago."

Casey was intrigued, but knew Aaron's flair for the dramatic, so she did not press it any further. However, Aaron was not through. He continued. "My guess is that there was no suicide involved. It was a triple murder. Tomorrow when you read about it the paper there will be mention of Mary Lou's lover and killer being in a blue Chevrolet that was found at the scene. The only problem is Mary Lou was admitting a man into her home who, like her, was being set-up by sinister forces intent on covering up one murder with three more. In the trunk of that blue Chevrolet was another man. The man managed to get into that large drawing room where he met Mary Lou and the driver of the car. He killed them both and the butler, probably stood right next to the guy driving the Chevrolet and put a bullet into his temple, placed the gun in his hand and then scurried out of the house and climbed over those short grey stone walls that surround the place. He was probably picked up by a confederate who was waiting for him. They dove away, thinking nobody is smart enough to figure out exactly what went down."

Casey, amazed at the deductive reasoning power of Aaron, was overwhelmed with admiration for a young man who seemed to never cease to astound her. "How did you figure all that out, Sherlock?"

Smiling, Aaron could not resist a bit of levity. "Elementary my dear Watson, elementary."

Casey replied, "OK, Mr. Sherlock Holmes, I admit it. You are some amazing detective."

"Hey, I am going to amaze you even more when we meet Gillie and Wild Bill to see what they found out about the older man standing beside Eric. Let's stop at a phone booth and call them. We'll meet at Hop's."

It must be remembered that Gillie, being out as a homosexual in 1963, was an anomaly of gigantic proportions, especially in the small town south of the Bible Belt, where those who flaunted convention were deemed offensive to God. So, when he walked into Hop's with Wild Bill to meet Casey and Aaron in their now self-designated "truth booth," the diners were appalled at his brazen feminine-looking clothes and brash disregard for convention. Typical of Gillie, knowing the people were disconcerted by his appearance and manner, he actually put on a more ostentatious display of femininity.

Wild Bill, by now, used to Gillie's flamboyant behaviour just shook his head, and having become aware of Gillie's expectations of being treated like a lady, stopped at the booth and waited for him to slide in first. Gillie looked up at him and said, "Why thank you big boy."

Wild Bill replied, "Stuff it."

Casey and Aaron found the pair cute. However, there were more pressing issues. They shared with them the information about the murder and then Aaron asked the question that would blow things wide open. "The photo?"

Wild Bill leaned over the table and whispered, "You know who it was don't you?"

Aaron could not resist. "Of course, it was Eric's dad, Franklin Parson. Am I correct?"

Gillie, shaking his head, replied, "You know you are right. You had it figured all the time didn't you? Now, tell us where all this is leading."

"The world is filled with people who cause great human and moral consequences by their lies, manipulation and thirst for wealth and power; also, because of their insatiable desire for carnal pleasures. That is what this entire sordid affair boils down to, the pursuit of carnal pleasure and its consequences when violence is used to achieve it. These people think they can do as they please with no consequences, and because of the way our political system is set up, they are generally right. Wealth and power equal either a free-pass or just a slap on the wrist. You see, Mary Lou made a statement about Mr. Parson being interested in her."

Casey's eyes lit up and she said, "Yes, I remember, Aaron. I didn't put much credence in it, because she seemed to just dismiss it lightly, calling him a creep."

Aaron continued. "Yes, she made light of it, as if she was disgusted by Eric's father. However, we both know she is a woman who is not above using her physical attributes to get that which she desires. I am convinced that she was having an affair with Eric's father when she was only 17 years old. That, in itself, was statutory rape, pure and simple. Even if Mary Lou was willing, the law says it is rape, because of her age."

An excited Gillie said, "So, Mr. Parson was having an affair with Eric's girlfriend?"

"He was." Then Aaron asked Casey a question. "Remember the smell of the perfume the day we went to visit Mary Lou?"

"I do, Aaron. I didn't think much of it then, but I think I know where you are going with this."

Aaron gave her a wink and continued. "I went home that night and my Mom noticed the residual smell from our visit with Mary Lou. She made a comment about me being out with a very rich woman, as no mere high school girl could afford *Essence of Pleasure* perfume. She recognized the smell, because my dad had bought her a one ounce bottle a few weeks before when they had a big fight and he had to grovel for forgiveness."

Again Aaron looked over at Casey and asked a question. "Remember what Rob Waterhouse said Sue Ann mentioned about he smell of her rapist?"

"Yes! Yes! She said he smelled like he was wearing women's perfume. Whoever raped Sue Ann had been with Mary Lou right before the assault. One highly likely person was Eric, but you think it was Eric's father, right?"

Nodding his head in the affirmative, Aaron said, "I do think it was his father; although, I am not 100% sure. You see, my guess is Eric knew about the dalliances between his father and Mary Lou, because he was and still is frightfully afraid of his father and will do anything to stay in good graces with him. In fact, I think he would even help him murder someone who might expose the fact that Franklin Parson was Sue Ann McGee's rapist and the father of her baby. They were both following her and Rob around for fear that the two of them might uncover the truth. Exposing Franklin Parson could destroy Parson Manufacturing. They had no idea that Sue Ann was going to have an abortion; and thereby, eliminate their biggest worry. They made the mistake of killing her only one day before she was scheduled for an abortion that might have ended the whole sordid affair then and there. My guess is there is a chain of people complacent in the murder and cover-up. Years of darkness are about to see the luminous truth, and we are the ones holding the flashlight that will shine on the truth."

Gillie, Wild Bill and Casey all recognized that they were witnesses to an exhibition of supreme genius at deductive reasoning. Aaron was a young man of superior investigative intellect who simply was at the very top of his game when pursuing the truth.

Wild Bill asked what their next move was, and Aaron replied, "We can't go to Chief Martin. Not only is he incompetent, but he is owned by the Parson family and the other wealthy interests that he relies on to keep his job. I am going to set in motion the public exposure of them all. It will be laid out for all to see, and there will be no denying that there was a conspiracy of silence in dealing with Sue Ann McGee's death. When I get through, the truth will be laid completely bare and there will be no way out for those who murdered Sue Ann and those who were complacent in covering it up."

Aaron got a forlorn look on his face as he continued: "I am not naïve enough to think they will pay much of a penalty, because the rich can afford the best lawyers and they get preferential treatment when sentenced by judges who reserve the harshest punishment only for the poor and the minorities. Even juries have more reverence and sympathy for the well-connected than for the poor. Still, we will see to it that there is a modicum of justice for Sue Ann McGee. These people will be exposed, and just maybe a smart lawyer will want to help the McGee's go after the Parson millions in a civil court suit for wrongful death. That is real justice anyway when it comes to the rich. Taking money from them is the highest form of punishment for the well-off, because money is at the heart of their very existence.' Aaron got up, smiled at his three comrades and said, "Let's rock and roll."

CHAPTER 11
THE GUY WHO JUST BROUGHT DOWN
YOUR EMPIRE

Life was a desperate and frantic struggle.
Cursed by my enemies, I endured unto death.
I was placed in the valley of eternal sleep.
Injustice was the epitaph carved onto my tombstone.
I rose from the darkness of the grave, seeking retribution.
A champion of justice embraced my cold body.
For me, he and his charges fought indifference.
The deceit was brought from the shadows into the light.
Only now can I finally rest in peace.

Aaron's distaste for the wealthy, double-dealing, fake sham artists in their mansions of arrogance had for years kept him on the path of righteous indignation toward those at the top of the economic order who protected their privilege at all costs. He could almost hear them shriek with rage as if he had poisoned their guard dogs, vaulted their protective moats of aloofness and crossed their finely manicured lawns of conceit in threadbare garments and the rags of a pauper to force open their thick doors of audacity and pretensions. He wanted to give the masses the fire from the burning torch of hope to heat their cold homes and light the streets of despair as he urged the poor and downtrodden to ditch their cuffs and chains. He wanted to make the lords and ladies in their palaces and castles shake with fear at the coming rebellion of the oppressed. This was more than a battle to get justice for Sue Ann McGee. It was a determined war against the privilege and arrogance of the fortunate, advantaged elite. Fighting the privileged was no easy task, and what Aaron was about to undertake was an audacious attack on the coddled, indulged and advantaged of Asheboro society.

So, the stage was now set for Aaron to bring down the high and mighty and lay bare all the facts that led to Sue Ann McGee's death. Casey and Wild Bill went to the *Randolph Picayune* newspaper office to share all the information they had accumulated with the editor, Tom Foreman, a man of integrity who had fought determined battles against the Asheboro establishment over the years. He had attacked the Ku Klan in the 1940's and early 1950's, when it used fear and intimidation against the African American population. He had come out in support of Martin Luther King's drive for civil rights. He admonished the school board for allowing religion to be forcibly taught in the schools, as he boldly proclaimed that freedom of religion should also include freedom from religion. He had fought against the mandatory recitation of the Pledge of Allegiance that blindly brainwashed children into supporting the government right or wrong. In fact, he had boldly printed the statement by that vilified icon of human rights, Che Guevara, that you should *support the country always, support the government when it deserves it*. Tom Foreman had steadfastly stood for liberty and justice against the forced compliance of the populace to a set of ideals imposed by those who thought that they knew what was best for the people of the community. He was specific in pointing out that those people who imposed their will were generally the elite of the business, political and religious establishment who justified oppression in the name of social order. He was indeed a man of great intestinal fortitude, dedicated to serving his fellow man, no matter what it cost him. And it often cost him dearly in terms of lost advertising revenue from those who vehemently disagreed with his defence of liberty and justice for all.

Tom was immensely intrigued by what the foursome had turned up in their incredibly judicious investigations. In fact, he said that he was a bit ashamed that he had not investigated Sue Ann's death more vigorously all those years ago when it occurred. He felt remiss in his duty to the community and to Sue Ann's parents. However, he was now prepared to headline in the next day's paper, *FOUR TEENS DISCOVER PLOT TO COVER UP MURDER.*

Meanwhile, Aaron was going to meet Gillie at the office of Eric Parson to lay out the facts that would bring down the Parson Empire of deceit. Yes, Aaron's partner for the day was little Gillie Gilbertson, the effeminate, swivel hipped flirt who would bat his long eyelashes at any willing or unwilling man in town. He was only five feet tall with green-hazel eyes. He had flowing locks of hair that cascaded down to his shoulders, with the thickness of a full moon. He was as dainty as a tulip blooming in the noonday sun. His tight-fitting mini-shorts gave maximum exposure of his shapely posterior that he could wiggle like a belly dancer in dynamic gyration before a crowd of adoring men. He wore thigh high strapped brown leather sandals that allowed maximum exposure of his bright red painted toenails. His chest was covered with flowing white silk and linen that had little cut-outs in strategic spots to accentuate his soft white, hairless skin. He sat in the chair by the window in Eric Parson's office with his legs crossed as if he was an axis of two converging rivers.

In his soft left hand, he held a shimmering pearl inlayed purse. This was the guy who was going to be by Aaron's side when he went into battle against the baron of brutality, Eric Parson. Oh my, what an unlikely pair!

As Eric's secretary stared at Gillie with disdain and disbelief, Aaron walked into the office and was, himself, overwhelmed at Gillie's appearance. He could not help but think what a thrill it must be for Gillie to finally feel that there were at least three people willing to accept him unconditionally and call him friend. For the first time in Gillie's life, he was finding approval by not only Aaron, Casey and Wild Bill, but through their embracing of him, others were now realizing that a person's sexual orientation and outlandish way of dressing should play no roll in embracing them for their depth of character. Oh, and Gillie was quite the character!

Eric's secretary said to Aaron, as she looked with raised eyebrows at Gillie, "I told your friend here, Mr. Parson is out until 4:00 PM, and I am sure he is too busy to see anyone."

Aaron smiled and said, "Believe me, he will see us."

Just then the phone rang. The secretary looked up at Aaron, held the receiver out to him and said, "A Miss Felton wants to speak to you."

Aaron took the phone and a smile crept across his face as he looked down at the secretary. Bubbling with excitement, Casey said, "Done Aaron. I am in Mr. Foreman's office now. After a few verifications, he will be publishing the story on page 1 in tomorrow's edition. He is going to deliver a proof to Sheriff Effrem tonight. At the same time, he is releasing the story to all the newspapers in Greensboro, Charlotte, Durham, Raleigh, all television stations in the state, the AP and UPI. Sheriff Effrem will have no other choice than to arrest Eric and Franklin Parson, probably eventually even Chief Martin and Miss Fields. According to him, this is one of the biggest stories he has ever covered in Asheboro, and it is all because of your tenacity."

Smiling, Aaron replied, "And because of the devotion to the cause of justice by three of the most wonderful compatriots a person could wish for. Tell Mr. Foreman, he should have a reporter at the Sheriff's office right away. My guess is that Eric Parson will be over there shortly to save himself by spilling his guts out. Goodbye my little intrepid gumshoe."

"Bye, my dear Aaron. We'll meet you at Hop's around five."

"You got it, girl."

Aaron, as he handed the phone to the dumbfounded secretary, could not help but smile with smug satisfaction as he said, "You are about to witness the crumbling of the high and mighty Parson empire. In the distant future, this will be a day you can tell your grandchildren about – the day a ghost destroyed an empire of greed and arrogance, a day when the mighty actually were brought before the bar of justice in a nation that coddles the rich, privileged and powerful while ignoring the plight of those who live in quiet desperation, begging for a crumb from the table of plenty. You better start looking for new employment."

Astonished, astounded and bewildered by Aaron's tirade of indignation, the secretary could only utter those immortal words, "You're a communist!"

Aaron could not help but laugh out loud as he said, "That's the typical response from all you prisoners of manipulation who have been brainwashed by a government that promotes fear to keep you in line. Today, it is the communists who are out to destroy America's superior way of life. Tomorrow it might be Hindus, Muslims or homosexuals."

Gillie uncrossed his legs, sat up straighter and pumped his right fist in support of Aaron's tirade and said, "Go, boy! Go! They all line up to turn their brains over to government, corporations and religion that keep them in bondage."

Aaron turned, gave Gillie a wink and smiled. At that moment, in walked Eric Parson, who was not amused at seeing the two teenagers in his office. "What are you two doing here? I have no time for you. Out now Aaron Adams and take that homosexual strutting peacock with you!"

Very calmly, Aaron replied, "I'll get out, but your next guest will be Sheriff Effrem, and I would suggest you need to prepare yourself for a charge of murdering Sue Ann McGee and the murder of Mary Lou Hinton and two others at her house.. Come on Gillie, strut your stuff out of this den of complacency, so this arrogant jerk can cow-tow to his father one last time before they are both sent up the river."

Eric looked over at his secretary and said, "No one is to disturb us, under any circumstances." He then turned to Aaron and Gillie and just pointed toward his office door. He hunched his shoulders and strode to the door, holding it open for Gillie and Aaron to enter first. He walked in behind them and sighed as he went over to his desk, laboriously pulled out his high-dollar executive's chair and took a seat. Eric was a defeated man.

Aaron, for all his hatred of the high and mighty, who ruled like the lords of the manor and enjoyed the luxuries of life like Middle Eastern potentates, could not help but feel a tinge of sympathy for a man who had lived a life of arrogant privilege for so long, but was now watching it crumble before his eyes.

Eric took a deep breath, reached up and switched on the tape recorder that was on a table beside his desk. He then turned on the intercom and said, "Miss Hartnell, please leave your intercom open, turn on your tape recorder and listen carefully to the conversation I am having with these two young people ."

She dutifully replied, "Of course, Mr. Parson."

Eric then said, "This is Eric Paul Parson and I am having a conversation with Aaron Adams." He then paused and made a gesture with his hand indicating he didn't know Gillie's name.

Looking at the recorder, Gillie said, "Gillie Gilbertson."

Eric then gazed directly and despondently into Aaron's eyes, as if he was actually relieved that the years of living in the shadows of a lie were finally coming to an end and that he could unburden himself from the crushing weight of despair. He asked, "What do you know?"

"I know it was your father who raped Sue Ann McGee the same night that he had been with your so-called girlfriend, Mary Lou Hinton, with whom he had been having an affair for some time. I know that you went over to Mary Lou's house in the trunk of that blue Chevrolet driven by a man you and your father set-up to take the fall for a double murder. Your father waited outside for you to kill the two of them. You jumped over the stone wall, got in the car and drove away, thinking that once again you had gotten away with murder. I know that you, no doubt, got Miss Fields, who lives a pretty high life on a teacher's salary to assist you in the murder of Sue Ann McGee, or at least to help cover it up. I know that Chief Martin was probably involved in the cover up. That about sums it up."

"You are right on all accounts for the most part, Aaron. However, I did not hide in the trunk. For once in my miserable life, I actually sort-of stood up to my father and refused to commit another murder for him. It was he who was in the trunk. I am the one who waited outside the stone wall. Also, you should be aware that my mother and my brothers were privy to what was going on ever since the rape of Sue Ann McGee. The abominable actions of my father were condoned by us all out of fear and attachment to the exalted positions, power and money to which we had become accustomed. To protect our privileged lives, we refused to expose his abhorrent, despicable, immoral, criminal behaviour. We are all evil, shameful and contemptible and deserve whatever is coming to us. You are to be congratulated for undertaking that which no one else had the courage to tackle. You and your band of teenage sleuths have uncovered an evil that has grown and festered over the years. It has been like a cancer eating away at me, destroying my life. It will now, finally, destroy the entire family."

Aaron was in absolute awe of the candour displayed by Eric Parson. He was amazed that he was actually feeling a tinge of sympathy for Eric, whom he abhorred. Aaron realized that Eric was also a victim. He was a victim of fear and intimidation by a father who had no moral compass, and produced progeny who were just as callous as he was. In their culture of self-aggrandizement and greed, all was permissible in the pursuit of money, power, privilege and pleasure. They were truly bad seeds in the garden of evil.

Aaron calmly leaned forward in the luxurious high dollar overstuffed leather chair that was representative of the arrogance of those at the top of the food chain and asked, "But why did your father rape Sue Ann?"

"Why does he do anything? Simply because he wants to do it. He has always been attracted to underage girls. One day we went into the Side Car Café. He held the mortgage on the owner's house, and he was behind on the payments. While we were there, he couldn't take his eyes off Sue Ann, who was working that day. He told me I shouldn't be fighting with her, but romancing her. He said what she needed was an older man to break her in for me. He was totally infatuated with her. So, he got drunk and simply raped her. End of story for him. He got what he wanted, as he always does."

Disgusted, Aaron said, "What about the murder of Sue Ann McGee? How was that facilitated and covered up?"

Eric, now seemingly more relaxed, as he continued to unburden himself, let out a faint sob as he fought back tears. "That was an atrocity of unmitigated evil to cover the crime committed by my father. He lived in constant fear. He had me following Sue Ann everywhere she went. Then, when Rob became friends with her, we got doubly scared. We were even considering eliminating him, but one day Sue Ann came to see my father right here at his office. She said that she had told no one, but that she suspected it was me who had raped her and that she was pregnant. That was all she said. She demanded nothing, other than indicating that he should know the depravity to which his youngest son had stooped, and that he should do something about me. He told her to get out of his office and if she spread any rumours about me that he would have her mom and dad put on the streets, because he knew the owners of the dilapidated barn that they were living in. My dad was fearful that Sue Ann would expose the truth when the child got older, maybe even demand that it bear the Parson name, share in the family bounty. It was an albatross around my father's neck. He knew that there was no statute-of-limitations on rape, so regardless of the number of years that went by; if she found out it was he who committed the rape; he could have been convicted of the crime.

Aaron interrupted with another question. "So, your father was off the hook as far as Sue Ann was concerned. She did not know it was he who raped her?"

"No, she suspected me because of all the trouble we had at school, because of my arrogance and vindictiveness, and my infatuation with her. The irony is that I was probably as much in love with her as Rob. She was adorable, and she stood up to me when no one else would. I was jealous of Rob and the affection she was showing him. I wanted that affection, but was not worthy of it."

Tears were flowing now. He was sobbing like a child. He put his left hand on his forehead as he lowered his head, trying to hide the fact that he was wiping away tears with his right hand. He looked back up and continued. "My dad knew Miss Fields. Hey, he knew every woman in town who would consider a liaison with him. He wasn't very particular with whom he cavorted. In her day, Miss Fields was not a bad looking woman. Anyway, he was visiting her at the gym office one day and noticed the list on the bulletin board of those who were to go up the grappling rope. At the top was Sue Ann McGee, and he was convinced that was the way to eliminate a problem that was causing him great consternation. I don't think Miss Fields knew about the murder plans, but I think that she thought I was the father of Sue Ann's baby, and she wilfully assisted in covering up the fact that she thought I had arranged her death. She has been well taken care of by my father over the years."

Aaron shifted his position in the chair and asked, "And what of Chief Martin?"

That ridiculous buffoon was also having an affair with Miss Fields. My father convinced her to use her charms on him to avoid any investigation. Martin knew what was up. All the signs were there for any idiot to see it was murder. You see, the night before, Miss Fields gave my father the key to the gym. He had me slip in, climb up the grappling rope and almost cut the rope in two where it was wrapped around the beam. I even left cut marks from the knife I used on the beam. Check it out. My guess is that they are still there as prominent as always. Martin never bothered to check the beam. This is a man who routinely beats up suspects, especially blacks, to elicit confessions. You think he would have any compunction about covering up a murder by the son of the most prominent, wealthy and influential man in town? Get real!"

Aaron could not help but share some information that Eric was totally unaware of. "The irony Eric is that all the murders and cover-ups were absolutely unnecessary. You see, Sue Ann McGee had scheduled an abortion for the very next day."

Eric, seemingly exhausted, sighed deeply, reached over and hit the rewind button on the tape recorder. After the tape rewound, he took it off the spindle, leaned over his desk and reached out, offering it to Aaron. Aaron got up, took the tape and said, "So, you going to the Sheriff and turn yourself in, or you want us to send him out here to pick you up?"

Eric, with a sinister-looking smile that showed no contempt, but relief, said, "Neither is necessary. He will have a lot of people to arrest. I am going to save him some trouble."

Eric reached into a lower desk drawer, fumbled around in it for a few seconds and took out a gun. Looking at Aaron and Gillie, who both were fearful he was about to dispatch the two of them, he said, as he held the gun in his right hand just above the desk, "Isn't it great to live in a country where it is easier to get a gun than a driver's licence?"

As he made the statement, he raised the gun to his right temple and pulled the trigger. Brain matter and bone fragments flew across the room making a sickening sound upon impact on the far wall as Eric collapsed onto the floor. He could now join Sue Ann McGee in the cold ground.

The sound of the gunshot reverberated throughout the offices of Parson Manufacturing. The secretary ran in and started screaming. Gillie sat in complete disbelief, almost in shock from what he had just witnessed. Franklin Parson, whose office was just around the corner from his son's, came barging into the office. He stood confused and bewildered as he gazed upon his dead son. Of course, Aaron was calm and collected. He said to all those in the room, "don't touch anything." He walked to the reception room, where a crowd was gathering and he saw Ellen Stutts. He said, "Ellen, call the sheriff, be sure it is the sheriff, not Chief Martin, and tell him that Eric Parson has just killed himself.

A series of gasps among the crowd could be heard as the enormity of what had just occurred began to sink into those gathered in the reception room. Aaron, still the calmest one there, returned to Eric's office. He looked over at Gillie, who was still sitting there in shock and motioned with his index finger for him to get up. As Gillie came toward him, Aaron said to Mr. Parson and Miss Hartnell, "We'd better all get out of here and close the door until the sheriff arrives."

Franklin Parson turned to him and said, "Who the hell are you?"

Aaron, in almost a whisper, replied, "I am the guy who just brought down your empire."

EPILOGUE
I CAN REST IN PEACE. THANK YOU.

Kindness is a language the blind can see
and the deaf can hear.
Even the dead can sense its power.

The next few days rocked Asheboro to its very core, but the good people of the town rose to the occasion as good people everywhere always do. They coalesced in their demands for justice. Of course, justice was never as swift and sure for the powerful and well-connected as it was for the powerless and poor. Also, the punishment was less harsh than that reserved for the average citizen. No doubt, the evidence was so strong that even a man of Franklin Parson's stature had to be convicted, but he would not get the death penalty like the poor. He would get twenty years to life and be out in ten or fifteen years. Miss Fields and the sheriff would get five years and be out in two or three years. The rest of the Parson family could not be convicted, because the evidence was too flimsy. However, the fallout from the scandal would lead to the demise of the Parson Empire and the family would flee far and wide from Asheboro, never to return again.

After all the turmoil, it was decided to hold a memorial service in the school's gym marking the tenth anniversary of Sue Ann McGee's untimely death. Planning to attend the services with his three comrades, Aaron drove his belching pile of junk car to pick up Casey. It was near sunset and the sky was painted a flowing crimson colour with fluffy clouds dancing about over the Uwharrie Mountains.

At the doorway, a vibrant Casey stood in anxious anticipation of Aaron's arrival. Aaron pulled up in front of the house and she motioned for him to get out. Her father stepped out onto the porch with her mother and enthusiastically greeted Aaron. Shocked, Aaron could hardly muster any words, other than, "good to see you, Mr. and Mrs. Felton."

Mr. Felton, with sincerity in his voice, said, "We are mighty proud of the fact you and our daughter uncovered such a dastardly foul deed. We are equally delighted that you and she are such good friends. We will be going to the memorial service ourselves, but we know the two of you probably have something planned afterward, so we will let you two go on and we'll see you at the school. We hope to see you around here often, Aaron."

"Yes sir. I would like that very much."

As the two of them walked to Aaron's car, Casey whispered, "You are in their good graces Aaron. Milk it for all its worth. I have heard nothing but praise for you the last several days. They think you are a great guy. And guess what, so do I."

Opening the door for Casey, Aaron whispered, "I don't believe it."

The two of them went by to pick up Gillie, whose mother came out to tell them that Wild Bill had come by to pick him up. She asked for a ride, and Aaron willingly consented, surprised at the simple way in which she was dressed. Gillie certainly didn't get his flamboyant style of dressing from her, he thought. Aaron considered that perhaps Gillie got it from his father, who had long ago deserted his family and condemned them to a destitute existence that left them on the fringes of poverty in a country with no real social safety net.

All 1200 seats in the gym were filled and folding chairs were set-up to make room for a couple of hundred more people. The guests of honour, Mr. and Mrs. McGee, Wild Bill, Gillie, Aaron and Casey were seated at the far end of the gym near the archway to the infamous corridor. After the opening prayer, which was mandatory at all public functions, the guests were introduced to rousing applause and each presented with an engraved gold medallion that stated: *Presented by the city of Asheboro in recognition of service to the community and furthering the cause of justice.*

Gillie, as always, was his flamboyant self, dressed like a courtesan visiting Louis the 14th at Versailles. He actually received a huge round of applause, no doubt for his sartorial splendour as much as for his devotion to the cause of justice. Wild Bill lumbered his bulking frame up to the dais and awkwardly accepted his medallion. Casey, dignified and alluringly beautiful, accepted with profound grace and made sure that she mouthed the words "thank you" to Aaron, for she knew it was he who had made all this possible. Aaron stood in humble humility as the crowd roared its rapturous approval when he was called up to accept his medal. It made him particularly proud to see his father, whose praise he rarely received, standing in the front row with his mom, both of them wildly clapping their hands.

After the closing statements, the crowd lingered for awhile, coming up to shake hands with the four heroes and Mr. and Mrs. McGee. It was a cathartic moment for all in the community, as the veil of deceit that had prevailed for so many years had been lifted.

Aaron and Casey agreed to meet Wild Bill and Gillie at the Blue Mist Café for a milkshake to celebrate. Watching Wild Bill and Gillie unabashedly holding hands as they exited the gym, the two of them stood by the entryway to the corridor. Casey reached down and took a surprised Aaron's hand as the janitors were busy sweeping debris from the floor. She pulled the mystified Aaron toward the locker room. She smiled at him as they entered and stopped in front of locker 23. She longingly looked up at him and said, "You have wanted to kiss me ever since the second grade. Don't you think it is time you did it?"

Aaron bent over and gently kissed her on the lips, ever so briefly. Casey slowly shook her head, almost in disgust, and said, "You call that a kiss?" She reached up, wrapped her arms around Aaron, pulled him snugly to her chest and pressed her ruby red, thick, moist lips to his. The kiss lingered for what seemed an eternity, as they melted into each others arms. Then the ecstasy was shattered by the sound of a shower behind the tiled wall. The two of them parted lips and began to gingerly walk back toward the shower. As they got behind the tiled wall, the shower suddenly ceased. With great trepidation, they looked over at the mirrors that were filled with foggy steam. On one of them, slowly dissipating as the moisture dribbled slowly downward, were the words *I CAN REST IN PEACE. THANK YOU.*

J. Wayne Frye

Other Aaron Adams Adventures:
Fall From Apocalypse
Armageddon Now
Something Evil in the Darkness at Hopkins House
When Jesus Came to Jersey as the Son of Thunder
The Girl Who Stirred Up the Whirlwind
When Jesus Came to Canada to Lead an Indigenous Rebellion
In the Broughton Archipelago

VOCABULARY BY CHAPTER
(Definitions relate to the usage in the context of this book and come from the Canadian Merriam-Webster Dictionary)

PROLOGUE

demise: death or end

disdainfully: without respect, to look upon with scorn

heinous: grossly wicked or reprehensible

distraught: deeply agitated or extremely upset

reverberated: to continue in or as if in a series of echoes

recriminations: accusation in response to one from someone else

wanton: maliciously or unjustifiably

paragons: a model or pattern of excellence

stoically: impassive; characterized by a calm

ostentatious: given to pretentious or conspicuous show in an attempt to impress others

promulgated: an open declaration, to let be known, open declaration

melancholia: an extreme manic depressive condition

reverberated: reflected, a series of echoes

CHAPTER 1

cusp: a point

fervent: having or showing great warmth or intensity of spirit, **feeling:** enthusiasm

persona non grata: Latin for "person is not welcome"

segregation: the practice or policy of creating separate facilities within the same society for the use of a minority group or groups

alluded: to make indirect reference

stratification: forming depositing, or arranging

subtle: so slight as to be difficult to detect or describe

adept: a highly skilled or well-trained individual

disdain: a feeling of contempt for someone or something regarded as unworthy or inferior

behest: an authoritative order or command

penchant: a strong and continued inclination

edification: instructive knowledge that makes things clearer

pretentious: making usually unjustified or excessive claims, generally in reference to one's importance

ignoble: characterized by baseness, lowness, or meanness/ of low birth or common origin

audacious: daring, reckless, bold

unmitigated: not lessened

exalted: raise or elevate in rank, power or character
cower: to shrink away or crouch - generally from fear
admonition: counsel or warning against fault or oversight
propensity: an often intense natural inclination or preference
apex: the uppermost point
loathsomeness: disgusting
brusque: rudeness by being short, as in a curt reply
raucous: loud and rough
dire: fraught with extreme danger, nearly hopeless, causing dread or terror
cataclysmic: severely destructive
sustenance: the act of sustaining life by food or providing a means of subsistence
metamorphosis: a striking change in appearance or character or circumstances
acquiescence: acceptance without protest
ostracized: to exclude from a group by common consent
hierarchy: the organization of people at different ranks
perpetrated: to perform an act, usually negative in nature
prudence: knowing how to avoid embarrassment or distress
atrocious: shockingly brutal, cruel or displeasing
affirmation: the act affirming or asserting the truth
unabated: being or continuing at full strength or force
pièce de résistance: outstanding item or event
insatiable: impossible to satisfy
vindictive: disposed to seek revenge, showing ill will with a desire to hurt
unabated: continuing at full strength or intensity
CHAPTER 2
adjacent: nearest in space or position; immediately adjoining without intervening space
throng: a large gathering of people
permeated: occurring throughout
solace: the act of consoling, to give moral or emotional strength
reverberating: a deep prolonged sound that reverberates
dissipated: disperse, disappearing slowly
translucent: almost transparent
spectre: a ghostly appearing figure
apparition: appearance of a ghostlike figure
portend: indicate by signs

quizzically: questioning manner
trepidation: a feeling of alarm or dread
dastardly: unprovoked, treacherously cowardly
foray: sudden and short attack, initial attempt, briefly enter enemy territory
untenable: incapable of being defended or justified
Lothario: a successful womanizer
enamoured: marked by foolish or unreasoning fondness
infatuation: foolish and usually extravagant passion, love or admiration
irrevocably: can't take back, stays as it is
defilement: to make filthy or dirty, debase the pureness, corrupt
havoc: violent and needless disturbance
CHAPTER 3
propagandized: promote or publicize a particular cause or view, attempt to influence
abyss: an immeasurably deep chasm, depth, or void
confidant: someone to whom private matters are trustfully shared
transcend: go beyond
malign: evil or harmful in nature or influence, to attack someone's character
inordinate: beyond normal limits, excessive
meticulous: marked by extreme care in treatment of details
undulating: move with a smooth wavelike motion
stratified: divide society into social classes or castes
simpatico: being on the same wavelength : congenial, sympathetic
foreboding: a feeling of evil to come
psyche: that which is responsible for one's thoughts and feelings
anomaly: deviation from the normal or common order or form or rule
echelon: a level of command, authority, or rank
nemesis: something causes misery or death
extol: praise, glorify, or honour
cannon-fodder: personnel regarded as likely to be killed or wounded in combat
compatriot: a colleague or very close friend who shares your ideals
fervently: having a lot of passion in regards to something
fervour: emotionally aroused and worked up
euphoric: exaggerated feeling of well-being or elation
altruistic: showing unselfish concern for the welfare of others
sublime: inspiring awe, worthy of adoration or reverence

surreptitiously: secret or unauthorized

pensive: expressing or revealing thoughtfulness, usually marked by some sadness

titillated: to excite pleasurably

malarkey: exaggerated or foolish talk, usually intended to deceive

comradeship: the feeling of closeness and friendship that exists between companions

laden: to put (something) on or in, as a burden

CHAPTER 4

squelching: to crush by or as if by trampling; squash

savior-faire: a polished sureness in social behaviour

utopian: founded upon or involving idealized perfection

ignominy: deep personal humiliation and disgrace

banter: to speak to or address in a witty and teasing manner

crux: a main or central feature

furtive: sly; shifty

tenacious: holding or tending to hold persistently to something

sedate: calm, dignified, and unhurried

CHAPTER 5

abeyance: the condition of being temporarily set aside; suspension or inactivity

maligned: to speak harmful untruths about; speak evil of; slander; defame

effeminate: having feminine qualities untypical of a man

abomination: a vile, shameful, or detestable action, condition, habit

inconsequential: lacking importance

penchant: a strong inclination, taste, or liking for something

intrepid: characterized by resolute fearlessness, fortitude, and endurance

gumshoe: slang for an investigator, especially a detective

mundane: common, ordinary, banal, unimaginative

caveat: a warning or caution

overwrought: full of nervous tension; agitated

effervescent: to show liveliness or exhilaration

impishness: of, relating to, or befitting an imp; especially mischievous

acuity: sharpness; acuteness; keenness

profusely: exhibiting great abundance, extravagance

stratification: the way in which different groups of people are placed within society

pariah: any person or animal that is generally despised or avoided
exuberant: filled with or characterized by a lively energy and excitement
levity: humour or frivolity
doted: to be lavish or excessive in one's attention, fondness, or affection
facade: a false, superficial, or artificial appearance or effect
circumspect: watchful and discreet; cautious; prudent
fidelity: the quality or state of being faithful
distraught: agitated with doubt or mental conflict or pain
quagmire: a difficult, precarious, or entrapping position : predicament
CHAPTER 6
debacle: sudden, disastrous collapse, downfall or defeat
henchmen: a trusted follower, generally for personal gain
scoundrels: mean or base in nature; villainous; dishonourable
donnybrook: an uproar, a free-for-all, brawl
inexplicably: Difficult or impossible to explain or account for
intrepid: characterized by resolute fearlessness, fortitude, and endurance
beguiling: charm or enchant (someone), sometimes in a deceptive way
sinews: source or mainstay of vitality and strength
reverentially: resulting from or showing reverence or respect
crème-de-la-crème: something superlative, very high in social order
riff-raff: persons of the lowest class in the community
dubious: questionable or suspect as to true nature or quality
awe-struck: full of wonder or amazement
edifice: a building, especially one of imposing appearance or size
Corinthian: elegantly or elaborately ornate or luxurious
ostentatious: characterized by or given to pretentious or conspicuous show in an attempt to impress others
gargantuan: gigantic; enormous; colossal
audacious: daring, adventurous, spirited
magnitude: size; extent; dimensions
sieve: shifter, sometimes refers to easy to pass through
interlopers: one that intrudes in a place or sphere of activity
audacity: fearless daring, heedless of restraints
flippantly: disrespectful, shallow or lacking in seriousness
atrium: a large open space within a building usually with a glass roof

tirade: a prolonged outburst of bitter, outspoken denunciation
dalliance: A casual romantic or sexual relationship
foreboding: Fearful apprehension; a feeling that something bad will happen

CHAPTER 7

precipitously: extremely careless or excessive
chagrin: keen feeling of mental unease, as of annoyance or embarrassment , disappointment or a disconcerting event
derogatory: disparaging; belittling, diminishing
judiciously: having, exercising, or characterized by sound judgment : discreet
discombobulated: disconcerted; upset; frustrated; confused
rebuke: to turn back or keep down
intuitive: based on what one feels to be true even without conscious reasoning; instinctive
insidious: treacherous or deceitful
culpable: deserving of blame or censure as being wrong, evil, improper, or injurious
bombastic: pompous, overblown,

CHAPTER 8

contrite: feeling or expressing remorse; affected by guilt
embowered: surround or shelter
repugnant: extremely distasteful; unacceptable
malaise: is a feeling of general discomfort or uneasiness; moral or mental ill-being
moonshine: illegally distilled homemade whisky
cogent: appealing forcibly to the mind or reason; convincing
quip: a witty or funny observation or response usually made on the spur of the moment
oblique: not straightforward : indirect
retroussé: turned up at the end (generally referring to the nose)
supposition: An uncertain belief
unequivocally: a way that is clear and unambiguous
germane: being at once relevant and appropriate
tenacious: persistent

CHAPTER 9

miscreant: behaving badly or breaking a law
coalesce: to unite for a common end; join forces
status-quo: maintaining things as they are
aghast: filled with horror or shock

ardently: warmth of feeling; passionate
affinity: an attraction to or liking for something
arduous: involving or requiring strenuous effort; difficult and tiring
clandestine: kept secret or done secretively
curry: seek favour by fawning or flattery
egocentric: total interest in self with little or no regard for others
whimsically: given to whimsy or fanciful notions; capricious
unscathed: without suffering any injury, damage, or harm
archaic: very old or old-fashioned
abysmal: extremely bad; appalling
indignation: anger or annoyance provoked by what is perceived as unfair treatment
cognizant: fully informed; conscious
steadfastly: fixed or unchanging; steady

CHAPTER 10

sanctity: the state or quality of being holy, sacred, or saintly
cathartic: purification or purgation that brings about spiritual renewal or release
nonchalant: feeling or appearing casually calm and relaxed
verbatim: corresponding word for word to the original source or text
anomaly: one that is peculiar, irregular, abnormal or difficult to classify
disconcerted: disturb the composure of; unsettle
flamboyant: highly elaborate; ornate; given to ostentatious or audacious display
credence: mental acceptance as true or real; credibility
grovel: begging in order to obtain someone's forgiveness or favour
luminous: brilliant intellectually; enlightened; well-lit
modicum: a small quantity of a particular thing

CHAPTER 11

epitaph: brief literary piece commemorating a deceased person
aloofness: .distant physically or emotionally; reserved and remote: stood apart
pretensions: aspiration or claim to a certain status or quality
anomaly: peculiar, irregular, abnormal, or difficult to classify
flabbergasted: to overcome with surprise and bewilderment
fortitude: courage in pain or adversity
tenacity: the quality or state of being tenacious; determined
intrepid: characterized by resolute fearlessness, fortitude, and endurance

dumbfounded: greatly astonished or amazed
potentates: one who has the power and position to rule over others; a monarch
progeny: a genetic descendant or offspring
atrocity: appalling or atrocious condition, quality or behaviour
statute-of-limitations: a type of law that restricts the time within which legal proceedings may be brought
vindictiveness: marked by or resulting from a desire to hurt; spiteful; revengeful
liaison: a close bond or connection : interrelationship; an illicit sexual relationship or affair
cavorted: apply oneself to sexual or disreputable pursuits
compunction: feeling of guilt or moral scruple that follows the doing of something

EPILOGUE

coalesced: come together and form one mass or whole
demise: a person's death; convey or grant
destitute: without the basic necessities of life; not having
courtesan: woman prostitute, especially one whose clients are members of a royalty or men of high social standing
sartorial: Of or relating to tailoring, clothes, or style of dress
dais: raised platform located either in or outside of a room or enclosure
rapturous: characterized by, feeling, or expressing great pleasure or enthusiasm
unabashedly: not ashamed, disconcerted or apologetic; boldly certain of one's position